Against the Storm

Against the Storm

Gaye Hiçyılmaz

A Yearling Book

To Muzaffer

·{ 1 }·

MEHMET did not understand how anyone could talk of going away in the spring. Spring was short enough: a few beautiful weeks between the melting of the last of the snow and the coming of a burning summer, when the waist-high grasses dried and rustled and scratched. Nevertheless, they were talking about going, and this time it was not other families — it was his own family.

The school year would finish in early May. "I can see nothing to keep us after that," said his mother. Mehmet could not believe it. Had his mother gone blind? Many of the women in the village drew scarves over their hair and mouths; now it seemed as though his own mother had pulled her scarf down over her eyes as well. He searched the faces of the other grown-ups. They nodded in agreement with his mother. Were they blind, too?

"Look at it." His father spread his arms out, and everyone looked out into the dusk beyond his outstretched fingers to the handful of fields, the flock of sheep and goats, and the copse of birch trees that no longer flourished because their land was drying up. In the distance, a good day's walk away, you could see the mountains where they always used to take the flocks at the beginning of the summer. That was what they always did as soon as school ended. They did not load their things into a truck and drive away into some town, even if the town was Ankara. Everyone knew that Ankara was the capital of Turkey. It might be very nice to go and see it. In fact their teacher had told them that it was their duty to go and visit it, but that did not mean that you had to go and live there — and in the spring, too.

In spring, in his village, the grass grew long and lush and green. There were flowers everywhere. Mehmet's little sister, Hatice, picked them by the armful and stood them in rusty tin cans all over their house. All the fruit trees in the village were in bloom, and in the evening the blossoms glowed. Each house was lit by the white of the pear and the plum and the pink of the cherry; the prettiest of all was the pink and white that nestled among the silvery gray of the apple trees. Last weekend Mehmet had helped his grandfather paint the trunks of their apple trees with white lime. It was to keep off ants and other insects, but he thought it made the trees look prettier than ever.

The baby lambs and kids born into the cold of winter were, by the springtime, straight and strong and ready to be played with. For spring was the time, above all, for playing. The snow and mud of winter were almost gone and with them the biting cold that kept even the toughest of them in by the stove. The heat of the summer that made you sweat and itch and seek out the shade of the drooping trees — that was in the future. Now you could run out of the house, stopping only to slip your feet into shoes, if you bothered at all about shoes. A couple of shouts would bring out a couple of boys, and by the time you had fixed four big stones for goals, you would have enough people around for a soccer game. When you had kicked the breath out of yourself and the ball, you could slip off and steal the unripe fruit from somebody else's tree. There was plenty to eat, too, with lettuces and spring onions to lay in your bread. And then there were extra eggs as last year's chicks came on to lay. The eggs his family did not eat Mehmet packed into a straw-lined basket and took down to the main road. People in big cars would stop and buy them. They also bought flowers — wild hyacinths and bluebells — if the village children made them into very nice bunches.

On warm, spring evenings the family sat outside, under the bright, bright stars, and his mother cooked the thin, soft bread called *gözleme*. She turned it once, twice, over the hot copper sheet, then sprinkled it with salt and folded it up; they ate it warm with the salt sharp on their tongues. Mehmet would listen to the talk of the grown-ups, and hear yet another one of his grandmother's stories about people who had tried to be smarter than her but had not quite managed it. Finally someone, his mother usually, would lead him off to bed, and he would be dreaming almost before she threw the soft, cozy *yorgan* over him.

3

Now they had spoiled it all. Mehmet's throat was so dry he couldn't even swallow the *gözleme*. It just stuck to his tongue in a doughy lump. He didn't feel sleepy either, for his grandmother was not telling stories this evening; she talked instead about going away, and so did the others. No, that was not quite true. They had been talking about going away for years, asking themselves if life wouldn't be better in the city and wondering why they shouldn't do what one of the family had done: Yusuf *Amca*, his father's brother, had gone away to Ankara years ago and come back in a red Mercedes.

Yusuf Amca was a rich man, and his children were pale and plump and always wore new clothes like rich people's children. They both went to secondary school: children got a better education in the city. There was not even a secondary school in Mehmet's village. Next autumn, when he would start secondary school, he would have to walk for an hour down to the town on the main road. It took two hours to get back in winter. Last winter one of the village boys had lagged behind the others in town; he'd missed the path in the snow and had frozen to death, just like that. He was the best goalie on the soccer team — it had been horrible. Mehmet had, at the time, said that he wasn't going to lag behind — he was going to keep up with the others. But his parents didn't listen to him. It was not only schools, they said. What about doctors? There was no doctor here. There was a woman who sometimes came round for babies and things like that, but she did not seem to be very good at it. Children's new brothers and sisters were always dying.

4

His family had talked and talked and talked, but now it was different. They had finally decided to go. The question they were now discussing was when. That *when* seemed to be coming nearer.

He could have told any of them that they were wrong: his father and mother, his grandfather and grandmother, his uncle and aunt who lived with them. He could have told them if they had asked him, but they did not. They never did ask eleven-year-olds, even if they were boys rather than girls. Mehmet could have told them that while Yusuf Amca's wonderful stories of apartments with electricity and water that always ran from the taps and big shops with thousands of different things to buy were true, there was another side to it.

He knew this because his best friend, Hayri, had written and told him. Hayri and his elderly mother and father had left the village nearly two years ago. It was for Hayri's sake that they had gone, for Hayri was clever. When he and Mehmet were in the third grade, their teacher had come one evening and explained to Hayri's astonished parents that Hayri was not just clever, he was, well, different. Now, it was true that Hayri was fair-haired and blue-eyed in a village where all the children were dark-haired and brown-eyed, but Hayri couldn't help that. Anyway, his grandmother had been a fair, blue-eyed beauty from another village, far in the west. Everyone, even his poor, gentle, worried mother was used to the fact that Hayri was the naughtiest child in the village. People said that it was because he was born too late. Mehmet's own grandfather laughed at this idea.

"It's a good thing he's naughty. It wouldn't be right for anyone who looks like an angel to behave like one, too. It would be tempting fate." That was what he said. Hayri's own, elderly, father mocked the neighbors for their complaints and said that Hayri, his tenth and last child, was a *süzme* child, a "strained" child, in the way the best yogurt is strained to get out the excess water. He did not explain further. Naturally, Hayri's white-haired father and anxious mother did not contradict the teacher.

Hayri's teacher was the same one who had taught their nine other children, and they respected his opinion. So when he said that in all his long years of teaching he had never taught a child as clever as Hayri, they believed him because they knew he would not lie, but his opinion did not make them happy. Hayri always did his homework in three or four minutes leaning against the wall whereas other students, like Mehmet, spent hours worrying over it. Hayri was like that, not because he was lazy, but because he was clever. He was not just more clever than other children. He was different from other children. His parents, who had provided more or less adequately for the other nine, now felt unable to provide for Hayri. The teacher said that it was a sin to keep him there in the village. He must go to a big town. There he could be prepared for scholarships to the best schools in the country. It was the duty of his parents to do something for this unusual boy.

So they had packed up and gone. One day Mehmet and Hayri had been out with Hayri's dog, trying to hit birds with slingshots, and the next day everything had been loaded into a truck and Hayri had climbed in, too, on top of the mattresses, and had waved good-bye. The truck had bumped away in a cloud of dust, and Mehmet had never seen Hayri again.

They had been friends since their first day at school. Hayri, who could already read and write, had helped Mehmet with his letters, and Mehmet had knocked down an older boy who called Hayri a girl because of his golden curls. After that things had evened out: Hayri had learned to fight as well as the next, and Mehmet had got the hang of his letters. This had only made them better friends. They had never spent a day apart.

So this unexpected parting was like a death, only worse, because it was somehow untidy. At least when the goalkeeper had died in the snow, it was finished and you knew where he was, even if he had been frozen blue and stiff. Mehmet had no idea where Hayri was. He didn't think he could have withstood the separation if it hadn't been for Hayri's dog, Korsan. Hayri had left Korsan in Mehmet's care until he came to fetch him. But Hayri had not come.

Hayri did send the village teacher a long letter, which the teacher read aloud in class. It was more like a book than a letter, and the teacher kept it in a plastic bag in the china cabinet in his house so that it wouldn't get dusty. Visitors were always shown Hayri's letter. That letter told them all about Ankara, and the teacher was very proud of his former pupil. Hayri wrote about his new school, too, although not in great detail. There were over sixty children in his class, and his new teacher hit them over the knuckles with a cane when they got an answer wrong. The village teacher just did a bit of hair pulling, hardly enough to make your eyes water.

Then, months later, another letter arrived at the village. This one was for Mehmet.

My dear friend,

How are you? I hope that you and your family are well. Please give my respects to your parents and grandparents. I miss you very much. How is Korsan? Does he miss me? Please keep him safe. I shall not bring him to Ankara — I do not think he would be happy here. I am still studying, especially mathematics.

Your loving friend,
Hayri

This letter was written on a page torn from an exercise book, and the envelope had been made from another folded page. His parents thought it was a very polite letter and beautifully written. But Mehmet could only think of all the things that the beautiful writing had not said. He felt uneasy and showed the letter to Korsan, who sniffed it and whimpered restlessly and stood in the doorway, waiting. Together they had walked around the village, following the paths that they had always followed with Hayri and remembering the adventures they had shared.

Mehmet never received another letter. Nor, as far as he knew, had the teacher. Everybody said that Hayri must be too busy with his studies. Mehmet doubted it: if things had been going all right, Hayri would have found some way of writing. You couldn't stop Hayri from writing. Some of the rocks around the village were still covered with his writing. Mehmet could have told all this to his family, but he didn't. He knew that they would not listen to him. Why should they when they could not even see all the things that were not in the letter? Even if he jumped out in front of them shouting, "Don't go! Don't go!" it would not help. They would push him aside, though gently. Grown-ups heard your words, but they did not listen to you.

So he sat quietly, watching the dark movement of the clouds over the shining moon and listening to their plans with deepening horror. The sheep and goats were to be sold — it was a good time now, after the spring grass. They would fell the birch trees later — who knows, it might yet be a wet year. The teacher wanted to buy their chickens. Mehmet bit down the nail on his thumb.

"I'll miss my chickens," said his mother. "What will we do with the scraps?"

"Yusuf says that there won't be space for chickens, not at first," his father said firmly; he did not like chickens.

"What about when we get a house of our own?" his mother persisted.

"Then, I promise you, I'll buy you a whole batch of chicks — scientific chicks, not your ordinary village hens. And I'll build you a scientific chicken house." Mehmet's father was full of promises — he always had been. Now he had a promise for every problem and doubt.

"Of course there will be work. There always is in the city." This he promised to Mehmet's Osman *Dayı*, his uncle from his mother's side of the family. Osman was

9

young. He was Mehmet's mother's youngest brother, and he, his young wife, Elif, and their baby daughter, Filiz, lived with Mehmet's family. Osman had everything: good health, good looks, a healthy daughter, and the prettiest wife in the village. Mehmet thought secretly that Elif could have been a princess, she was so lovely. Osman had everything, except work. He had no land of his own — well, he had two fields of mainly stones. He had worked as a pastry cook in the town, but times were so hard nobody spent money on pastries, and for the last year he had not worked. So Mehmet's family had squeezed together and had taken them in. Osman Dayı was so cheerful and Elif *Abla* was so beautiful and lively that nobody had minded, Mehmet least of all. Osman Dayı had promised to teach him to shoot, and Elif, who was not much older than Mehmet's elder sister, Ayşe, was always ready for a game or a joke. It had seemed a good arrangement to Mehmet, and so he had been surprised to overhear Elif say, "I won't go on living here like this," with her pretty mouth turned down and tears in her eyes.

"There'll be work in the city," promised Mehmet's father. "Trust me. Think of Yusuf Amca. In no time at all, you'll have a little home of your own. Elif might even find a job. Lots of women work in the city." Elif's eyes, which were the color of honey, started to glow. She could already imagine her house with green velvet curtains — that was what she had always dreamed of: green velvet, from floor to ceiling.

There had been promises for everyone — that is, everyone except Mehmet. Nobody seemed to think about him.

They just assumed there would be a school somewhere for him. He thought that it must be because he was not special like Hayri. . . . He would just be packed up, along with the pillows and the saucepans, and driven off to Ankara.

··{ 2 }··

IT WAS THE VILLAGE teacher who finally mentioned the problem that Mehmet had been avoiding. Mehmet had been thinking about it; he had lain awake at night worrying, but he had the feeling that if he talked about it, his family would make a decision, just like that, without even asking him what he thought. Now it was the last day of the school year. Mehmet had got his school report, which was all right, although nothing like the reports that Hayri used to take home. He had come to the teacher's house to say good-bye and kiss his hand, and to give the message that Osman would bring the chickens over early in the morning before they left. He didn't add that his mother hoped to get a few last eggs out of those chickens.

"Thank you, my son," said the teacher. "I've told my wife to clean out the chicken house. Each time we eat an egg, we will think of your dear mother and be thankful."

It didn't seem as though Mehmet himself were going

to be remembered at all. The old teacher shook his head.

"It's a very big change for you, isn't it? Don't worry. I expect you'll do all right."

The teacher didn't sound very sure of himself. In fact, he sounded tired and anxious, and Mehmet knew that he had not said anything like that to Hayri. He had called Hayri's going-away the "first step on the glorious road to success," and he had begged him not to forget his first, humble village schoolteacher. He had also given Hayri a letter of introduction to the teacher of his new class. Now he smiled without meeting Mehmet's eye, and his wrinkled fingers flicked his prayer beads round and round on their string. Did he know something more about Hayri? If he did, he was silent, and Mehmet waited for him to say "good luck" or at least "have a good journey," but all he heard was the *click, click* of the yellowed beads. Mehmet was already turning to go when the teacher called out after him: "Tell Osman that he can bring Korsan over tomorrow, too."

Now the problem was out in the open. Mehmet dared not say, "But I'm taking Korsan to Ankara with me," though it was true. Instead he nodded and touched the old man's hand quickly to his forehead and ran off. So that was what his family planned to do — they planned to leave Hayri's dog behind with the teacher. He was not even their dog. He was Hayri's dog. He had never even been Mehmet's dog — everyone knew that. Korsan always came to meet Mehmet from school, but he never followed him home until he was quite sure that Hayri was not somewhere inside the school building. Well, he was not going to pass the message to Osman. No, somehow

13

or other, he would get Korsan to the city. His mother might be persuaded to give up her chickens, but he would never be persuaded to abandon Korsan.

Korsan was an Anatolian shepherd dog, a *Kangal*. He was a powerful, creamy white dog who stood elbow high beside Mehmet. He had been bred in another village, and generations of his family had guarded the flocks of sheep and goats. They had fought off wolves and bears in the mountains and wild dogs and thieves on the plains. Korsan's ears had been cut short soon after his birth to save them from being torn in fights, and this gave him a sad, puzzled expression. Korsan, however, had never worked as a sheepdog. He had been given to Hayri when he was still a little puppy. They had grown up together. Hayri, with his angel's face and the charm of the devil, had always got presents as a little boy. People said he could have squeezed water from a stone. At one time, before Hayri started school, Korsan had been much bigger than Hayri, and Hayri had ridden the dog like a pony. Time had evened that out, too. Hayri and Mehmet were taller now, but Korsan was much stronger than both of them together. Mehmet did not think that there was a part of the village or its surrounding country that they had not explored, just the three of them, and they had had adventures, too.

He remembered the time when Hayri had fallen into the river. That was before either of them had learned to swim. Korsan had plunged in and dragged Hayri back to the shallows. They had taught themselves to swim after that, but Korsan could always swim better than either of them. They had never told anyone about the accident and

14

had been stony-faced when questioned over Hayri's soaking clothes.

Another time they had got lost on a chill autumn evening. They had been out looking for berries when a thick mist followed by a moonless night had caught them far from home. Mehmet could still remember the sound of other things out in the night, moving yet unseen. They would never have found their way back home without Korsan, for the homeward path led through rocky outcrops with sudden deep crevices and slides of pebbles that could send you tumbling over and over to the very bottom. They were met by the searchers just beyond the village, and this time they could not pretend that nothing had happened. Mehmet had been shouted at a lot and beaten a little. Hayri's mother had sewn a prayer into a little bag and put it round her son's neck. Hayri's father had spat and slapped his thigh and kissed them all and had sent somebody down to the butcher to get a big marrow bone for Korsan. Then he had roared at them, too, and said that they were never, ever to leave home without Korsan again, and they never had.

Unbelievably, Hayri's parents had taken him to the city and left Korsan behind. It made it all the more unreasonable of Mehmet's family to expect him to abandon the dog now. He wouldn't. He might not be special like Hayri, but he could do some things, too.

It would not be easy. Korsan was obedient; if you told him to sit, he would sit, and if you told him to stay, he would do that, too, for hours till you told him to come. The trouble was, he was huge. It was not like trying to take a tortoise with you in secret.

15

His family had been trying to load up the truck all day, and when Mehmet returned from the teacher's, they were still working. It did not look as if there were enough room for Mehmet alone and certainly not with Korsan as well, especially in secret.

"Leave it! Leave it! You don't need this rubbish — leave it, woman!" His father, bossy and bad-tempered, was unloading bundles on one side. Elif, a devilish twinkle in her eyes and her headscarf slipping from her long chest-nut hair, was slyly passing the bundles round the back of the truck to Mehmet's mother, who was fitting them in again on that side. Osman squatted on his heels and whis-tled like a bird and looked the other way.

"You don't need that," said Mehmet's father, peevishly kicking a big red plastic basin and making all the plates and tea glasses inside it shudder and clatter. "I'll get you a new one. I'll get you a washing machine in the city. We'll have to do things differently there. Leave it behind, I tell you."

"Until you get that washing machine I can see an awful lot of dirty clothes piling up," said Mehmet's grandfather in a tone that expected to be listened to. "Take it!" he ordered. Mehmet's father, who had had enough of load-ing up anyway, threw up his hands in despair and stalked off to the *kahve*, the coffee house, to join the other men. Everybody breathed a sigh of relief. He was not a very practical man. Now they stood in silence and looked at the truck and the remaining bundles on the ground. They had not got much for a family of eleven, but it was clearly more than one truckful. This gave Mehmet his chance. In that quiet and depressing moment when they all realized that it was not going to work out, Mehmet touched Osman on the arm.

"Couldn't we go later, by bus?" he whispered. "We could take the extra things with us." Osman smiled at him. Mehmet saw his advantage and pressed on.

"Elif Abla would like it." Osman seemed convinced. Everyone knew there was nothing he would not do for his wife. And Mehmet remembered hearing Elif say she wasn't looking forward to being bumped around for hours on end with a load of furniture and children. And Osman had agreed — he liked things to be dignified. Mehmet knew that he had to put his brilliant idea into action before his father came back.

"I'll go and get the tickets now, if you like. Suppose we are waiting on the main road tomorrow and the bus doesn't stop for us." It was a horrible thought.

"But it'll be dark before you get back," said Osman, who knew that he ought to go and get the tickets himself.

"That doesn't matter — I'll take Korsan with me. It will be our last walk together, after all."

Osman gave him the money and instructions that two of the seats were to be good ones, at the front and not over a wheel. An hour's walk took him down to the small town that lay along the main road to Ankara. The man who sold bus tickets had shut up his office and gone to the *kahve*, but he came with Mehmet and they studied the bus plan together. Mehmet would have liked to step back: the man smelled so sour, and his desk and papers were covered with ash that had blown from the heaped

17

ashtrays. The man pointed to two vacant seats on the plan, and another little gray pile tumbled down from his trembling hand.

"Just three of you, is it?" he asked.

"Three and a baby, a small one." Mehmet coughed and added, "And a bit of luggage — bedding and things."

"Bedding we'll take, and babies, especially small ones, but no goats. They stink and then I get complaints. You have no plans to bring a goat?"

"No, I've no plans to bring a goat." And Korsan? Suppose at the last minute they said "no dogs," because dogs smell a bit, too, especially in hot weather?

"I have vacant seats on the nine o'clock, two at the front, but the other is right at the back, you wouldn't want that . . . now, here's just the thing: three together on the twelve o'clock."

"I'll take the nine o'clock. We have to leave early," said Mehmet. Three seats together did not suit him at all. He decided not to mention Korsan. The man might say no now and warn the driver to be on the lookout for them in the morning.

"Can you ask the driver to pick us up at the bridge?" The man lit a new cigarette from the glowing tip of the old one, took a long pull of the filthy smoke, and handed the tickets to Mehmet. It must be a bit dull, Mehmet thought, always writing out tickets for other people to go to new places and being stuck in this grimy office yourself.

It was a strange thing, but once he had those tickets safely in the pocket of his jacket, he felt excited. Setting out was different from going away.

When he got home, nearly everything had been packed

18

up. It no longer looked like home. Mehmet found that they had packed his bed in, by mistake, but he said that it didn't matter — they could leave it where it was. He settled down in the straw in the deserted stall and rested his head on Korsan's firm shoulder. It was better like this. He wanted to sleep lightly and be up with the first light.

Nobody slept well, and they were all up very early, stiff and cold in the dawn and sipping sweet, black tea that still tasted bitter. It was very, very quiet; anyway, what was there to say, now that they were going? Mehmet's father and grandfather climbed into the front of the truck beside the driver. Then his mother and grandmother and Ayşe Abla and the little ones, Hatice and Ali, scrambled into the back. Osman fastened up the tailgate. The lights of the truck came on. Then its engine turned over once and then twice. The brake came off with a long sigh, and slowly they rumbled down the road. Elif tipped a bowl of clean water after them, so that their journey might be as easy as the flowing of water, and then they were gone.

Now Mehmet's heart beat so fast that he had to swallow back the bitter tea that came into his mouth. He must be careful. He disappeared back into the stall and waited there until he saw Osman set off with the chickens. They dangled from his hand like feather brushes. When Elif was busy with the baby, he slipped off quietly, with Korsan at his heels. Then he ran. He ran panting until he came to the birch wood. "Sit! Stay!" His voice was shrill and breathless, but Korsan eased himself into the grass and lay down.

"Stay, Korsan. Stay!" Oh, please, please let him stay. Then he ran back. Osman returned smiling; the teacher had been asleep so he had been able to put the hens straight into the chicken house and return at once. Nobody had remembered Korsan. Mehmet sat on the bundles and played with the baby and never breathed a word.

A neighbor came with a donkey and loaded it up. Osman pulled the door shut and picked up a couple of bags. Elif rolled the baby into a blanket and flung her best green silk scarf around her hair. Mehmet swung the last roll of bedding onto his shoulder, and then they were off, too. Perhaps the others had been right and spring was a good time to leave. Osman strode ahead whistling and joking with the neighbor. Elif hurried behind on her tiny slippered feet with her best flowered şalvar, or trousers, swinging out behind her. The sun had risen, and the dew sparkled in the grass. As they passed the birch wood, a breeze rustled the fresh green leaves, and Mehmet, lagging behind, called Korsan softly to him. Please, please let no one look behind. He thought that Elif did look once, and their eyes met, but she never said anything. That was like Elif. She had her own plans and was not so interested in what other people did. Or maybe she had not seen Korsan at all.

In their rush not to be late, they were much too early. Mehmet left the path before the bridge, calling out that he knew there were wild strawberries on the banks above the water. He said he would pick some for the journey. Korsan, hidden by the bridge, lapped greedily at the icy water. The river was deep now, swollen with the melted snows of the faraway mountains.

"Mehmet!" Elif's voice floated down from the bridge. "Mehmet, the bus is coming!"

It worked as he had hoped it would. The bus driver complained about the amount of luggage. Passengers got down to make sure that nobody stole their things. Elif worried that somebody might be sitting in their seats.

"Osman Dayı," said Mehmet, "I'll watch the bundles and things. You ought to take Elif Abla and the baby into the warm bus." Osman climbed thankfully into the bus; it was true, Elif's hand in his was freezing. The bundles were stowed away. As the driver was climbing back into his seat, Mehmet pulled open the high back door.

"Korsan!" he shouted over the running motor. The big bus was throbbing.

"Korsan, quick!" With great bounds the dog came out of his hiding place and started up the steps of the bus.

"Hey," cried the conductor, who was young, "what do you think you're doing?" As the bus gathered speed, Mehmet and Korsan reached the top step together. Passengers hastily drew in their legs and put their hands behind them, for country people are cautious of strange dogs.

"Where do you think he's going?" asked the conductor in a quarrelsome manner. Mehmet said nothing. He drew slowly from his pocket the money that his grandfather had given to him on the last *bayram*, or holiday.

"Big dog like that . . . he ought to have a ticket. . . ." The boy looked sulkily at the money. Mehmet drew out another bill.

"He'd better be quiet," the conductor muttered. "I'll

kick him off if he's not quiet." And he put the money in his pocket.

"He'll be quiet," said Mehmet. He'd done it. By the time they got to Ankara, it would be too late! He squeezed into his place by the window, and Korsan curled up as small as he could under his feet.

All seemed to be going well until suddenly the loud music was turned down and the bus swung off the main road onto the crunching gravel in front of a large garage. Mehmet had not known that the bus would make a stop. The conductor announced that there would be a stop of fifteen minutes and that all the passengers might have a glass of tea in the restaurant as the guests of the bus company. There was a rustle of newspaper as people got out bread and cheese and homemade pies. Children fussed on being woken from their sleep, and the old man beside Mehmet began to ease his feet back into his shoes. Suddenly Mehmet saw Osman pushing his way down the crowded aisle to come and get him. The color drained from Osman's handsome face when he saw Korsan. Then it came flooding back, and he looked at Mehmet in embarrassment.

"Are you crazy?" he muttered. An interested crowd of passengers gathered, peering over the backs of the seats at them. "Get rid of him. Send him back!"

"I can't. I couldn't leave him. Osman Dayı, don't make me. He won't be any trouble, I promise you." Then, without intending to, he was crying. The tears were streaming down his face, and he was wiping his nose on his jacket sleeve like a really small child. Osman, who had no more bad temper in him than a kitten, for all his fierce, black moustache, looked around at the other passengers for help. He hated quarrels. He hoped that somebody else would force the dog off. He did not want to be blamed for forgetting to leave the dog with the teacher. Then a man at his elbow nudged him.

"Fine dog, that. He'd get a good price in the city."

"That's right," said the man's wife. "They're very fashionable — I read it in the paper. People in society want them as guard dogs."

"Yes," said another woman, "you can never be too careful." And she fingered her gold bangles as if she wished that she were in society. The passengers' sympathy had wavered and turned in favor of Mehmet and the dog. Osman felt it and smiled at them. It had never struck him that Korsan might be valuable in the city. Korsan lay still, though his dark eyes were open and watchful and he did not sleep again but raised his head from time to time to be sure that Mehmet was still beside him.

Mehmet knew that Turkey was a big country, although he had never traveled beyond the town on the main road. Now he was astonished that they could drive on and on, sometimes through small villages, sometimes through very big towns, and then ever on again, along a road that never stopped. The empty land flowed into hill after hill, and after each downward slope of the road, there, in the shimmering distance, was the outline of another hill. It never ended, and when they finally reached the busy streets of Ankara in the early evening, he guessed that the road must go snaking on into the warm night.

The terminal was thronged with people and loud with

23

the coming and going of coaches. Porters, street sellers, passengers, beggars, soldiers — they all darted here and there. Mehmet saw several families like his own, standing bewildered next to their heaps of luggage, not knowing which way to go or what to do next. The baby whimpered, and Osman brought out the scrap of paper with Yusuf Amca's address on it: Number I, *Yokuş Yolu, Şentepe*. It sounded a nice enough place: Number I, Steep Way, Happy Hill — if only one knew where to find Happy Hill. The scurrying crowd of people who knew where they were going ebbed and flowed around them. Osman began to show the address to anyone who would stop. They read it and murmured the name to themselves: "Happy Hill." Then they shook their heads. They had heard of a district called Happy Hill, but they were not going there themselves, and they did not know how to direct Osman to the right road. There were, they said, a lot of hills around Ankara. They handed back the paper and hurried off along the streets that they were sure of.

The baby cried, and Elif pulled the scarf right over her face so that only her darting, curious eyes could be seen. Korsan stood with hanging head and drooping tail. Mehmet stared in amazement; when you have known every face in your village, it is disturbing to suddenly know none. The other passengers from their coach had melted away into the crowd. They shuffled closer together, feeling as if they were in everyone's way. Then Elif pulled Osman's arm and nodded toward a line of taxis. Several drivers said that they would not go that far out of town. One said that he would go, but he wanted half of all the money that Osman had left in his pocket.

24

Another, grumbling, agreed to go for less, but changed his mind when he saw Korsan. Osman cursed quietly.

Mehmet felt that he must do something to make up for all the trouble that he and Korsan had caused. He ran from person to person, showing them the address and begging them to tell him the way to Happy Hill. Everybody had something to say, but their advice was so confusing that he couldn't follow it. Finally, an old woman said that she was going that way herself, by *dolmuş*, or minibus. If they liked, they could follow her. But how could they manage the walk to the *dolmuş* park with so much luggage? Panic seized them. Osman, white with fury and wounded pride, bent down so that Mehmet could heave the great mound of bedding onto his back. The old woman looked impatiently behind her and started off. Elif picked up some bags and held them in her arms, together with the baby. Mehmet got hold of all that was left. Now he had no free hand for Korsan, and as they tried to get across a dreadfully busy street, every car on the road seemed to be honking at them. Even Mehmet wished that he had not brought Korsan. The old woman pressed on. Osman was strong and used to carrying heavy loads, but the pace and humiliation of this ridiculous race made his face twist with pain.

In the end they got to the *dolmuş* park. The old woman showed them where they must wait and then scuttled away to join her own line. It was already evening, and at least a hundred people were waiting in front of them. Each time the long line shuffled forward, they had to shift their things. People bumped into them and tripped over all their bundles. The sweat was running down Osman's face, and Mehmet had a feeling it was not just from the effort of carrying that heavy load. Osman resented being made to look absurd. He had told Elif that Yusuf Amca would probably be waiting for them with his red Mercedes. Mehmet, making himself as small as possible, had noticed that he and his uncle were the only men wearing the black şalvar of country people. He could tell that Elif was looking at the other women, who nearly all wore stockings, or even trousers, like men.

When their turn finally came, the driver was kind, in spite of his loud voice that had a strange accent. He jumped out and helped Osman rope everything onto the roof. His own home was near where they were going, he said. He patted Korsan's head and told them to get into the backseat, since theirs was the last stop on the run. Mehmet's spirits rose, and he pressed his face close to the window. He wanted to see everything in the city. And he hoped that he might see Hayri. He should be easy enough to recognize with his bright gold hair.

·{ 3 }·

THEY RECOGNIZED Yusuf Amca's house by the red Mercedes and the sound of his raised voice through the open window.

"I've told you before, but I'll tell you again, and this time don't you forget it, my girl — I like two and a half spoonfuls of sugar in my tea, not two and not three, but two and a half!" Mehmet heard a girl's voice, but it wasn't protesting. He stole close to the window and peered in. Yusuf Amca was sitting with his trousers rolled up to his knees and his feet in a basin of water. His wife, Fatma *Teyze* was pouring a kettleful of steaming water into the basin. His daughter, Yasemin, who was about the same age as Mehmet's sister Ayşe, was bringing another cup of tea. There was no sign of his own family.

"Be careful, woman — do you want to burn me?" came Yusuf Amca's sharp, rather high voice. He wore a shirt and tie and a vest. From the vest pocket he drew out a pair of spectacles, polished them carefully, and began to

27

read the paper, nodding to himself in a pleased way. He moved his feet about in the water, rubbing them gently against each other, and smiled to himself. It was a very nice room, with red chairs and a matching red carpet. There were a lot of shiny little black tables with lace mats and glass ashtrays on them; altogether it was a very shiny room.

"Osman Dayı, you go in. I'll just wait outside," said Mehmet. He and Korsan would be sure to knock something over in a room like that. He moved around the corner of the house and squatted down in the shadows with the dog. His uncle's house seemed larger than the surrounding ones. It was a square, one-story house with a red tiled roof. Mehmet was sitting in what was obviously a garden. There was a newly dug patch with spring onions coming up in a neat line, and beyond that something small and green that might be parsley. It was difficult to see, for the shadows were rapidly deepening. In the village, the coming of dark brought quiet and stillness, but here, there was incessant noise. Children were laughing and shouting, and babies were wailing. And there was the noise of music, the same music, but coming from all different directions. Then he realized that in many houses all around the people were watching the same film on television: a film with rolling music and gunfire in between. In the distance a dog started barking, and then, one by one, as though they were passing messages, others answered.

Korsan moved restlessly, and Mehmet felt the hackles rise up along his back. Suddenly there was a scampering of pattering paws, and some dogs, almost unseen but barking loudly, fled by in the dark. He waited on. He could hear snatches of conversation from inside the house: his uncle was telling them all what to do. Someone, somewhere, was still working; he could hear the *bang*, *bang*, *bang* of a hammer driving a nail into wood. There was a sudden burst of angry, quarreling voices, and from the town that stretched below them rose a roar that rolled up on the evening breeze.

Somebody breathing heavily came running unexpectedly around the corner of the house and tripped over Mehmet. Caught off balance, Mehmet went sprawling in the dust with the other person on top of him. They picked themselves up, and the boy, who was about his own age, stepped back in alarm when he caught sight of Korsan.

"Here, keep that great dog off me! Keep him off or I'll tell my father!"

"He won't hurt you — really he won't."

"What are you doing here anyway? This is Yusuf *Bey*'s house," said the boy, patting the bricks as though he had built the house himself. He backed farther away from Korsan, and as the light from the red room fell on him, Mehmet recognized Yusuf Amca's son, Hakan. Hakan had only been to Mehmet's village a couple of times and had stayed with the grown-ups, stuffing himself on the sweet cookies that had been baked for the guests. Mehmet's mother had called him a milk-pudding child. He was older than Mehmet, but only by a year or two.

"Sorry," said Mehmet, dusting off his trousers with one hand and keeping the other on Korsan.

"It's you?" said Hakan. He made a snorting noise, then added with a sly grin, "And are you really the last of

29

them?" Well, at least Mehmet now knew that the rest of his family had arrived. Fatma Teyze, hearing Hakan's voice, came fussing out of the house.

"Hakan, dear, where ever have you been so late? You're sweating! Now, come straight in and change your shirt and your vest or you'll catch a cold. Your father will kill you if he catches you out at night like this." She pushed him toward the door without seeing either Mehmet or Korsan. "Your father is not in a good temper as it is, not with all of them arriving like that. But he's soaking his feet, and you know that makes him feel better. I knew it would be like this, but your father knows best. He wouldn't listen to me, and now look what has happened; they've packed up and come! Hurry, Hakan, before you catch a chill. You know how sensitive you are — ugh!" As Korsan moved in the shadows, Fatma Teyze gave a little scream, and her hand flew to her chest. And then she gave another start as she saw Mehmet as well.

"Mehmet, how you frightened me! I thought you were a thief, hiding there like that. Whyever didn't you come in? Your uncle won't bite, you know, which is more than can be said of that great brute of yours. Keep him well away from me. I can't stand dogs. They're dirty, dangerous things, bringing in filth and diseases. No, on second thought, we won't tire your uncle any more, will we?" She was very short and wide and had a mouthful of winking gold teeth. "No, don't you bother to come in, Mehmet. I was just going to show Osman where we've put your family, so you can come straight along with us." She patted Hakan's plump pink cheek.

30

"Go in, dear, and change that shirt. You know you're just like your father — sensitive to drafts." It was surprising that anyone as small and fat as his aunt had enough breath to keep talking for so long.

They followed Fatma Teyze for three or four minutes along an unpaved road. She stopped in front of what seemed in the night to be the skeleton of a house. It was not really a block of apartments, but a very narrow building three or four stories high. Its base was so small that it looked to Mehmet as though it were leaning over him. It did not seem to have been finished, and their shoes scraped and rang on the rough brick steps of the stairwell. Through the gaps where the windows should have been, Mehmet saw that there were no stars in the cloudy city night. There were no high houses in his village, and he found himself holding on to the back of Osman's jacket as they went up the steep stairs. His aunt, panting from the climb, still managed to talk.

"Your uncle hasn't quite finished this, but he doesn't mind if you stay here for a little while. People have been begging us to let them have an apartment, but of course, we had to tell everybody that you were coming. We thought you would be happiest on the top floor. There's such a lovely view — you can see Ankara Castle on a clear day. It's very healthy to live high up. . . ."

His parents, grandparents, and his brother and sisters had laid their mattresses down on the bare concrete floor and had tried to stick newspapers over some of the empty windows. Kneeling on the floor, they were eating some of the *gözleme* that Mehmet's mother had made in the village. Fatma Teyze smiled in a superior sort of way and raised her eyebrows, as though she would never have settled down like that but understood that some people did.

Then she pinched Elif on her cheek and said, "Now, my girl, I know how newlyweds love to have a little place of their own. Come with me and look how nice this is. Your uncle said especially that Elif and Osman were to have this side!" She took them to the other side of the stairs and showed them an even smaller room, with one tiny window through which a cold beam of light fell upon a pile of newspapers, broken bottles, and moldy fruit skins that some other family must have left behind. Elif looked in and bit her trembling lip.

Despite his tiredness, Mehmet did not sleep well. He awoke several times to see the glowing end of his grandfather's cigarette as the old man sat by the window and smoked silently. Mehmet dreamed of seeing Hayri, of finding him among a group of schoolchildren who were having lessons in a room full of red armchairs. Just as he was hurrying to catch Hayri's sleeve, he saw that it was Hakan and not Hayri, and yet he was not as astonished as he should have been. He awoke to find his mother shaking his shoulder.

"Mehmet, wake up. Hakan's here. He's going to show you where the grocer's shop is. His mother sent him specially. Get up. Here's the money for some bread and a bottle of gas, a little one." Hakan did not come into the room. He looked into it from the doorway; he stared at the untidiness of the mattresses and tumbled clothes and he raised his eyebrows just as his mother had done. Then he turned his back on them and leaned against the doorjamb and whistled in a breathy sort of way, with no tune.

The two boys went out into the bright sun, Korsan following silently at Mehmet's heels. Hakan eyed the dog with a mixture of jealousy and fear.

"You'll have to get a license for him. He'll be shot otherwise." He looked with satisfaction at Mehmet's startled face and then explained that all dogs had to have a tag with their number on it to show that they had been vaccinated against rabies. Mehmet knew that this was true. He and Hayri had always taken Korsan down into the town to get him his injection, but this spring he had not done it, and here he did not know where to go. They were not idiots in the country, as Hakan seemed to think, but things had been different there. Still, he figured he could manage — and without Hakan's help.

He looked at Hakan's fat pink neck above his neatly ironed white shirt and at his black hair that was combed and parted just so. He was wondering if he could stick out his foot and trip Hakan up, when a battered plastic soccer ball sailed through the air and hit his cousin slap in the face. A roar of delighted laughter told Mehmet that he was not the only one who disliked Hakan. A group of ragged boys, dusty, sunburned, and stripped down to their shorts and dirty vests, fell about laughing and slapping each other on the back crying, "Good shot!"

Mehmet expected that Hakan would at least kick the ball as far away in the opposite direction as he could. Instead, Hakan dabbed at the blood that dripped from his nose onto his clean shirt and shouted, "I'll tell my father about you!" A very tall thin boy, who looked as though he had been stretched and whose head seemed to be

33

longer than it should have been, came up and put an arm around Hakan.

"I'm frightfully sorry, Hakan, dear. I quite forgot that you were so delicate." They went off to their game, this time choking with laughter.

Mehmet, without thinking, kicked their ball back to them. It was a long straight kick and went right to the feet of the tall boy, who looked back as if seeing Mehmet for the first time. Mehmet smiled, and the boy grinned back. Sometimes, when Mehmet thought about it all later, he thought that if he had not kicked that ball back, things might have been different. But how can you know that at the time?

"You'll see," hissed Hakan, "I'll tell my father about it." He sniffed loudly. "I'll tell him about you, too."

Within a week they had settled in. His mother said determinedly that she was used to "making do." She, Elif, and Ayşe had moved things around and in no time had the half-finished apartment looking much more homey. Winter was a long way away, and surely long before then the men would have proper work and the family would have moved into their own home. In the meantime, Mehmet's father would help his uncle out until something better turned up.

Yusuf Amca took them around one evening and showed them all the plots of land and houses that he owned. He had been steadily buying land since he first came to the hills many years ago. He was a rich man now. He told them they could forget about their rent until the autumn. Then, if they could afford the rent they could stay in the apartments permanently. And if they couldn't? Well, what was a few months' rent between brothers? Mehmet trailed unwillingly behind on this evening tour. It looked like showing off to him. His uncle, with his little quiff of white hair sticking up in front and his chest thrusting importantly against his striped vest, strutted exactly like a rooster. They were following him like a crowd of shabby hens.

"I could see how things were moving. I could see that one day these empty hills that nobody wanted would be worth a lot of money," crowed Yusuf, nodding to left and right as people greeted him respectfully.

Mehmet was surprised how quickly he himself settled in. He soon got to know the faces in the neighborhood, and, of course, people got to know him quickly because of Korsan. There wasn't another dog like him. His parents had been nicer than he expected about the dog, and for this he had his grandfather to thank. On that first evening the old man had said that he, at least, was glad to see a face that he knew! Perhaps the others felt the same way; anyway, there had not been much of a row. In secret, however, Mehmet worried about Korsan. He knew that he must have him vaccinated and get that tag, but he also knew that their money was melting away like last year's snow in the first sun. He had given all of his own money to the bus conductor.

In the end, it was the tall, long-headed boy, the one who had teased Hakan, who helped him. One evening, Mehmet was watching the soccer game that took place every evening on an open bit of stamped-out ground. One

35

of the players, lamed by a mean, low kick, limped off, and the tall boy, remembering Mehmet's straight shot, called to him to join the game. As he walked out onto that small patch of earth, he knew how the real soccer players must feel when they faced the howling crowds of thousands in the real stadiums. Some games are awful: you miss every shot and even trip yourself up. Some games catch fire: your feet have a feel for the weight and movement of the ball and you are always a stride ahead of everyone else in the game. For Mehmet it was one of those games. He made two goals, and there would have been a third if the goalie had not been so quick. When the game ended Mehmet knew that he had been accepted by the boys. Muhlis, the tall boy, explained that though he worked during the day, he was free in the evenings. Maybe they could kick a ball around together, he said.

"Well," said Fatma Teyze to Mehmet's parents after she had seen him playing soccer with Muhlis, "I expect you know what you're doing, but I wouldn't let my son spend time with that Muhlis." She would not explain because, as she always reminded them, she did not approve of gossip. Muhlis did not seem to have anything wrong with him, except that he was an odd shape. He was all ankle and wrist, but that could have been because his clothes were much too small for him. Anyway, Fatma Teyze should have been the last person to criticize — she had no shape at all!

The two boys found that they had more in common than soccer: just as Mehmet had his worries about Korsan, Muhlis had a horse to worry about. By coincidence, the horse didn't belong to him either; it belonged to his older brother Ramazan, who was away doing his military service. Muhlis was looking after both the horse and the business until his brother came back.

"What kind of business is it?" asked Mehmet. Whatever it was, it did not seem to be doing very well, because Mehmet had seen his new friend pick up pieces of fruit from the gutter, then polish them on his sleeve and eat them with enjoyment.

"I buy things — things that people don't want."

"Why do you buy them if people don't want them?"

"Well, then I sell them again to people who do want them. I buy used clothes and sell them again to a place in the city. I buy newspapers and sell them by the kilo as scrap paper. Bottles, glass, iron, even furniture. My brother used to deal in carpets. He'd swap them; he'd give people a new machine-made carpet, and they would give him their old carpets." It sounded like a funny sort of business, so it was not surprising that Muhlis looked hungry. In Mehmet's family they did not have clothes that they did not want. When somebody finally stopped wearing something, it was cut up into thin strips and woven into floor mats. He'd often helped in the evenings, cutting up the stiff cloth until his fingers got blisters, while his mother and sister sewed and sewed, winding those cloth snakes into heavy balls. But perhaps Muhlis's business wasn't so stupid; Mehmet recalled how he had sold eggs and bunches of flowers along the main road outside his village. Motorists had stopped and paid him money when they could have picked armfuls of flowers, free, if they had only got out of their cars and walked a little.

"You'd be surprised," said Muhlis, laughing. "Look at

your aunt. She swapped their old carpet for that new red one. That was some time ago. Today she won't open the door to me, pretends she doesn't know me. But I know her and I know her dear, delicate fatty!" He laughed loudly, but Mehmet was not sure that he completely understood the joke.

Yusuf Amca's land and property, including the half-built block in which Mehmet's family was living, was on the farthest edge of the shantytown. Years ago it had been just hills — softly rising bare hills. You could not *give* them away then. Their hill, or, more realistically, Yusuf Bey's hill, was called Şentepe. It dropped down to a stream, and then beyond the stream stretched empty land that formed part of the great Central Anatolian Plain. Mehmet had heard about it from Hayri, for Hayri had been the only person in their village who read books. He had had books bought for him the way other people have trousers and shoes bought for them. Even the schoolteacher didn't buy books, although he always read the difficult newspapers. Once Hayri had ordered so many books from a bookshop in Istanbul that the mailman had complained to Hayri's father about the weight of the packages when he had delivered them. History books were particularly heavy. The only time Hayri had kept still was when he had lain in the shadow of a tree and read and read. And then was so engrossed that he wouldn't have noticed if the tree had been cut down! Sometimes he had read bits aloud to Mehmet, and so now Mehmet could tell Muhlis about the Mongol hordes who had swept out of the eastern lands of China on their swift ponies. They had galloped over these rolling Anatolian plains. Their hooves might have thundered over the earth right here as they rode on and on until they were stopped by the sea, far in the west. Muhlis, who looked a bit like one of these Chinese riders, with his slanting brown eyes and his long, flat face, said that that must be why his horse, *Yıldız*, or Star, liked grazing there on the edge of the plain: she could tell that there had been horses there before her.

When they walked out to see Yıldız one Sunday morning, she tossed her head and threw out her forelegs as she trotted up to them. Mehmet, who was used to horses, could see that she had been a pretty thing once. A few men had kept horses in the village and looked after them better than they looked after their wives — at least that was what his mother always said. They had been fine-boned horses — brave, dancing creatures; they were not used for heavy work and drudgery. They were for riding out on a fine spring day, when you could look at the girls working in the fields and hold a frond of sweet grass between your teeth. At the touch of your heel they would break into a gallop, and often there would be no stopping them. He and Hayri had fallen many times. But now for a moment Yıldız halted, seeing Korsan. They saw a shiver run over her poor thin body, but then she tossed her head again and came on gamely. Muhlis put his arms round her drooping neck and buried his face in her mane.

"One day," he murmured, "when business is better, I'll get a new young horse, and then I won't have to work Yıldız so hard. I'll feed her on nothing but oats, and she'll retire, the way soldiers do." He brought a tidbit out of his pocket, and she nuzzled it from his hand and pushed against him for more. "My brother says that soldiers can retire quite young and still be looked after for the rest of their lives. Grow quite fat, they do."

"Is that what your brother is going to do?"

"No, not him, he's just doing his military service — he's not a professional." Muhlis bent down and looked at Yıldız's hooves. "No, it might be all right for an animal, but getting fat with nothing to do wouldn't suit my brother. Ramazan is going to do something — we're going to do something together when he gets his discharge."

The softer flesh inside one of Yıldız's hooves was swollen, and they noticed that she kept her weight off it.

"She's a bit lame," remarked Mehmet. Faraway on distant hazy hills, he thought he could see a village with red mud tiles and a minaret of paler stone. It could have been his village, but he knew that it wasn't. And it could have been Hayri beside him, but it wasn't. And he knew that the tired horse would never gallop unless you whipped her. But Muhlis was more of a dreamer than you would have expected in somebody who dealt in rubbish.

"She could have been a champion," he said. "She still is a lovely horse. You wait and see her in a month when she's had the spring grass inside her. She'll be quite frisky then." Mehmet nodded. He knew what Muhlis meant. But as they moved the stake so that Yıldız could graze a different circle, Mehmet was surprised at the thinness of the grass, for this should be spring.

"It's always been like this," said Muhlis. "Perhaps it was those Mongol horses, the ones you told me about. Perhaps they grazed the grass away and left us just the dust."

"It must be hard work, looking after her," said Mehmet. Muhlis nodded, pointing to her hoof.

"I ought to take her down to the veterinary place and get her hoof looked at. We could take Korsan and get him his injection, too. It's dangerous to leave it."

"Do you really think we could?" said Mehmet gratefully. He was going to ask Muhlis about Hayri and about finding the place where he lived, but he didn't. He felt awkward. It seemed disloyal to his new friend.

··{ 4 }··

THEY PUT off going to the veterinary clinic,
although they were both uneasy about their animals. Yıldız was lame and her fetlock was hot and swollen, but they couldn't get her treated until they found the
money to pay for the visit. Meanwhile Mehmet was
learning the patterns of life in the shantytown and finding
his own place in it. In some ways it was like life in his
village. If you didn't want trouble, you kept out of people's way, you didn't mess up your clothes more than you
could help, and you offered to do easy jobs straight away
before they asked you to do something awful like visiting
Fatma Teyze. Mehmet often helped by looking after the
younger children; he liked them and didn't mind watching them for a couple of hours. With them he could play
the sort of games that were babyish but still fun. In secret,
he loved Elif's daughter, Filiz. Filiz was a red-cheeked,
sturdy toddler, the sort of child who laughed rather than
cried and who liked to be tossed about and tickled. He

was teaching her to ride Korsan and was happy to play with her when Elif was busy with something else.

Mehmet had learned that keeping out of trouble in Şentepe meant keeping well away from Fatma Teyze and even farther away from Hakan. Mehmet's elder sister, Ayşe, had not learned the lesson. Hakan couldn't keep his hands off food. It didn't matter what it was, and as long as you could eat it, Hakan always wanted it. First thing in the morning, he'd call over the boy who sold *simit*, the delicious bread rings coated with sesame seeds. He'd take his time choosing the biggest and the softest one, and then he'd eat it slowly and wouldn't give away a crumb. It went on like this all day if he had money in his pocket — and he usually did. He would sit on the wall and call over everyone who sold something to eat. He'd buy the circles of papery, sweet *gofret*, or wafer biscuits, the sticky diamonds of cake, oozing with syrup, and the newspaper cones of salted marrow and sunflower seeds. In the evening he'd wait for the man who sold little skewers of grilled lamb intestines and for an old woman who sold spicy sausages that she made in her washbasin at home. He would eat huge slabs of greasy, rancid pie and dripping slices of watermelon. He wasn't fussy.

One day Ayşe and Mehmet were sitting on the wall with Hakan and his sister, Yasemin, watching some younger children who were pushing a plastic tractor through the dust at their feet. Mehmet's little brother, Ali, had the tractor now: he backed it carefully around a broken bottle and made squeaky engine noises, for his throat was dry and even though he maneuvered with care, the dust blew up into his face. A man with a pushcart of fresh, young cucumbers was coming up the street. They all heard him call, "Cucumbers! Cool, cool cucumbers! Crunchy, crunchy cucumbers!"

Only Hakan called the man over and bought two. The man peeled them and rolled them in salt and handed first one and then the other to Hakan. They watched Hakan and heard his teeth sink into the pale green flesh with a firm crunch. He chewed. It was a warm evening. Ayşe saw Ali stop driving as his eyes followed the movement of Hakan's jaw. She saw him try to moisten his lips as his eyes rested on the uneaten cucumber in Hakan's firm, white hand. She saw him open his mouth and swallow as Hakan bit and chewed again. Without a second thought she laughingly leaned over and took the second cucumber from Hakan. She broke it, *snap, snap,* into three and gave the pieces to Ali and the two other little ones. For a moment Hakan did not move. His face flushed red. Then he hastily stuffed the rest of the cucumber into his mouth and gave Ayşe a push that sent her backward off the wall. Yasemin giggled. Ali took the cucumber out of his mouth, as though he thought he ought to give it back. But Ayşe jumped straight up and slapped Hakan twice so that you could see the print of her hand on his pushed-out cheeks.

"You pig!" she shouted. "You greedy pig, I hope you choke on your food!" Mehmet was as surprised as the others. He would have done exactly the same as his sister, but Ayşe had seemed so grown up since they had come here that he wouldn't have expected her to get into a fight with an idiot like Hakan.

At home later, neither of them mentioned the quarrel,

but Hakan obviously had: the next afternoon their aunt came round to drink tea with their mother, and she watched Ayşe in a sharp sort of way. Hakan had come, too, but he loitered by the door and wouldn't come in properly, or go out either. Mehmet knew from a glint in his mother's eye that he would have to stay around as well. Mehmet and Hakan leaned on either side of the empty door and listened to the chatter of the women within.

Mehmet was surprised to hear Fatma Teyze complaining that Ayşe had been fighting with the neighbors. Mehmet knew only of that stupid fight with Hakan.

"Well," said Fatma Teyze, "these things do happen. She's a big girl, and you know what they say: 'The lazy brain plots trouble.' We could help if you would allow it. Why don't you let her come to us? It would do her good."

"Go to you?"

"Not in the house, dear, though I could do with some help, but in the workshop, where they do the sewing. Her uncle would always make an exception for her, as she is a relative. I mean, there is normally a long list of people wanting to work. You've seen it yourself. I can't leave my house without somebody begging me, imploring me to ask Yusuf to take on their son or daughter." It was true. Mehmet had seen it. He had seen a woman kissing his aunt's smooth hand, which smelled so strongly of lavender cologne; he had seen her kissing it and touching it to her forehead and pleading with Fatma Teyze to take her daughter into the workshop as a seamstress.

"You think about it," said Fatma Teyze, giving Ayşe a pat on her behind. "I'm sure that she's not really a bad girl. With a little firmness, she'd soon learn how to behave herself. We can't have one of our relatives fighting in the street like a gypsy!" She handed her glass to Ayşe to be refilled. Mehmet thought that if he had been filling it, he would have spat in it, quietly, but Ayşe was much too dignified for that.

"Yusuf Bey and I have been very lucky with our children but you know what they say: 'The stick comes from Heaven.'" She sipped her tea. "Then of course, we didn't have so many. . . ." And she smiled disapprovingly at Hatice and Ali.

"Do they really hit you with a stick?" Mehmet asked Hakan across the gaping hole of the door.

"What do you think?" said Hakan, and Mehmet wasn't sure. You could almost imagine him bursting open at the seams of his pale blue trousers at the first slash of the stick. The thought of Yusuf Amca with a stick in his hand was not pleasant.

"Shall we go out?" Mehmet's legs ached. "We could take Korsan for a walk." He hated this hanging about by the door because he knew that if you weren't careful you could see into the opposite room, where Elif sometimes slept beside the baby. Hakan grinned and shifted his position so he could spy on the sleeping young woman. He said that he was quite happy where he was. His mother, overhearing, said that Hakan was not to go out in the afternoon sun — he might get overheated. And turning to Mehmet's mother, she added that in the cooler evenings, he got chills — he was very delicate.

The afternoon dragged on into the evening. Mehmet could hear the shouts of the boys getting a soccer game together. The visitors seemed to be staying on purpose. All the time they stayed, the little trickle of gas under the teapot became weaker and weaker. After they left, there was not enough gas to cook supper properly.

It was their first miserable meal, and Ayşe made it even worse. She was the quiet and practical type, who never made trouble and always did what she was told. She usually sat by the window with Elif while they sewed together. With their fine, flying fingers they made pictures of birds and flowers with their colored silks and threads. But on this evening Ayşe pushed back her plate of half-cooked macaroni and buried her face in her hands and cried. Mehmet tried to think back to when he had last seen her cry; once, in the village, she had burned her blouse with the iron. He remembered it now. She had cried then, but Elif had lent her one of her own blouses, and she had dried her tears and laughed at herself for being careless. Here, there seemed to be no such easy solution.

"Don't make me go to work for them," she begged her parents. "I won't go. Please, please don't make me."

"I can't see the harm in it," said her father. "It's a good opportunity. We didn't leave the village so that you could pick fights with people. Lots of girls work in the city — I see them every day. It is not as if you'd be working for strangers."

"It's worse, much worse. I'll scrub the floors for strangers if you ask me to, but I won't work for them!"

"Whatever do you mean?" her mother asked, but Ayşe couldn't or wouldn't say.

"You don't know what you're saying, my girl," said her

47

father, looking angry and confused. Yusuf was, after all, his older brother.

"I'm working there, and if it is good enough for me, why isn't it for you?"

Ayşe's eyes were stubborn and unyielding. Her father looked down, then tried another approach.

"I don't know anything about tailoring, but you do." He came over and put his arm around her and tried to raise her chin. She looked up slowly, and he wiped her eyes with a corner of her scarf, which was pink and edged in a tumbling row of pink silk flowers. It was her own work. "Your uncle told me this morning that you've got a talent for this sort of thing. He said that city girls haven't got the patience of you country girls. Now, do it, just to please me."

She didn't smile; she thought for a moment and then said, "All right, I'll go, but I'll go because you asked me to, and not because of anything that Fatma Teyze said."

"There's a good girl," said her father. He kissed her on both cheeks and then began to whisper excitedly with Mehmet's mother about how much Ayşe might earn. Mehmet was not sure which of them had won that dispute. People said of Ayşe, "Still waters run deep."

Now, Elif was another matter: Mehmet thought he'd like to see anyone try and force her to do something she did not want to do. Elif never cried. She'd toss back her long braids, suck in her cheeks, and raise her chin in that firm upward movement that means no. And no it would be unless she saw a very good reason to change her mind. But not Ayşe. Grandfather called her his little dove, but gentle doves were famous for their steadfastness, too.

"There's my pretty girl," said her father, beaming and chewing through his lumps of half-cooked macaroni as if they were soft and tender. He liked to look on the bright side of life.

"You'll see, everything will be fine. I promise you. Trust me, Ayşe. Have I ever let you down? Have I ever broken a promise?" He had, of course, but nobody was going to spoil the restored calm by saying yes, least of all Ayşe.

Mehmet wouldn't have minded having a look at the workshop himself. His father said that there were about ten girls in one room with sewing machines. In another room there were two men who were the real tailors and who did the cutting. Mehmet's father did the heavy work: the moving of the bales of cloth, the loading and unloading of the vans, and the sweeping up. He didn't describe it very clearly, and Mehmet, having no idea of anything like that, didn't find it easy to imagine someone who had plowed his own land now sweeping up scraps of material from somebody else's floor. Mehmet sensed that his father didn't want to be questioned too closely. No, he wouldn't have minded having a look, but he had other plans, and he didn't want anything to get in their way. There was something about Hakan and his family. They reminded him of plump spiders: you needed to keep clear of their sticky webs.

Ayşe started work the next week and took some of her embroidery with her. She came home tired but satisfied. Everybody had said that her work was exquisite and that she had a real gift. The woman in charge of the sewing girls had said she was really sorry that this week there were only straight seams to be sewn. Later, who could tell?

"There, what did I tell you?" said her father, counting the money that Ayşe had brought back. She had given some to her mother and some to her father but had kept some herself, and Mehmet could see that his father didn't like that but didn't dare to say so.

Mehmet and Muhlis went to see Yıldız every evening. A neighbor had looked at her leg and had given them something to bathe it with, but they knew that they must get her to the vet. Then, one Saturday morning, Mehmet was woken by Korsan pushing his heavy head at his shoulder, just as if he were a sheep.

"Meh-met, Meh-met!" It was Muhlis calling up to him from the street, trying to be quiet and loud at the same time. He was waving a letter and looked excited. Mehmet jumped over the others, who were still sleeping, and ran down the stairs.

"I think it's from my brother," said Muhlis, with his slit eyes open as wide as they would go.

"What do you mean, 'think'?"

"Like I said . . ." Muhlis looked away and threw a stone for Korsan.

"Your brother is called Ramazan, isn't he?" Muhlis nodded and tossed another stone, and Korsan went after it in great bounds.

"You can read it if you like," said Muhlis offhandedly, as if he weren't even interested in the letter now. It was only then that Mehmet realized that Muhlis could not read.

The writing was in big, careful capital letters with a lot of erasures.

My dear brother,

I hope you are well. I am well and am counting the days until my discharge. Here is something that you may need. I have been working in the garden of a colonel. Give Yıldız a kiss from me and look after each other. Soon I have my leave and I'll be with you as soon as I can.

Your loving elder brother,
Ramazan

Muhlis took a piece of colored paper from inside his pocket and showed Mehmet several very new bills, which had been folded into it. It was obviously the money that his brother had earned gardening.

"We can go," he said happily. "We can go to the vet now, and Yıldız will be well again before Ramazan comes back."

"But I haven't got any money."

"I've got enough for both now" said Muhlis laughingly, and tossed another stone for Korsan.

The veterinary clinic was on the main road just outside the city center. They walked the whole way and worried that it would be closed before they got there. They didn't want to hurry Yıldız. They passed from the mud tracks of

51

the shantytown onto the noisy tarmac road. Yıldız, who was used to the town traffic, walked quietly and never flinched. Great strong Korsan cowered and cringed behind them, swerving from side to side with every passing vehicle. He frightened them both, until Mehmet took off his shirt and made a leash by tying one sleeve round the dog's thick neck. Then they got on better.

The porter at the gate grumbled and said they were too late. Muhlis saw a lady in a white coat and called out to her. She came over and smiled at them and told the porter to let them in.

"Don't I know this horse?" she asked, feeling Yıldız gently all over. "I'm sure I do."

"I never brought her in to you, though I know I should have," said Muhlis. "A lovely horse like her should be looked after. But it's not easy." He rubbed Yıldız's nose gently.

"I know it's not easy," said the veterinarian. Mehmet watched her carefully. He'd never seen a lady vet, though people said there were lady doctors in the city hospitals.

"Yes," she said. "I have seen this horse before." She was feeling along under Yıldız's belly, and now that Mehmet looked closely, he could see a long scar and the marks where the skin had been stitched together.

"I knew it — I never forget a patient." She smiled and rang a bell. The porter came scowling in, and she ordered four teas.

"I knew there was something about her the minute I saw you outside the gate. She looks a lot better than when I last saw her."

Muhlis went all red with pleasure at this praise.

"Did you buy her from a coal carrier?"

"My brother did. She's my brother's horse. He bought her from the coal man. I'm just looking after her until he comes back. He'll be back soon." Muhlis showed her the letter. "I've got the money to pay," he said. "I really have." He showed her that, too.

"She'd fallen," the vet recalled. "It was a winter afternoon. It was below freezing — I remember it well — the streets were like glass. She'd slipped on the ice trying to pull a load that was much too heavy for her. She'd fallen, and the cart's shaft had splintered and gashed her badly. They came and fetched me because it was just along the road from here, on that slope up to the Meteorological Station. I did my best for her, but I wasn't at all sure she'd recover. It's the worst of all lives for a horse here in Ankara, pulling carts of coal. I see more horses killed hauling coal than anything else."

"When my brother bought her from the coal man, she was still very sick. That's why he could afford to buy her. They thought she'd die, but my brother knew better. He said that everything ought to have a chance." He turned to Mehmet. "We had her in the house, you know, and we looked after her like she was human. I told you she was a lovely horse." The tea came, and the porter sat down with them to drink his. He acted as though he thought the vet was spending too much time on a couple of boys, but she took no notice. She told them what to do for Yıldız and gave Muhlis an ointment for her. Then she gave Korsan his anti-rabies shot and handed the precious tag to Mehmet, who put it in his pocket.

"Here!" the porter interrupted. "That's no good. That

53

dog has got to wear it or he'll get shot, sick or not!" Mehmet knew that the man was right.

"I'll get a collar as soon as I can," he said. "I promise." He meant it.

"Promises aren't any good," said the man sourly.

"Now, look here," said the vet. "He's a beautiful dog, and we don't want him to get shot any more than you do. Take this collar — it belongs to the clinic. We use it for stray dogs that are brought in." She showed him how to slip the tag onto the ring on the collar.

"But I can't take it. My mother would be angry."

"Come now, this isn't charity. I quite understand how your mother feels. But this is different. Your mother may not know that there has been an outbreak of rabies in Ankara. You know what that means." Mehmet did. He had seen newspaper pictures of people shut up in barred rooms in special hospitals, people who had been bitten by a rabid animal and would never come past those bars alive. It was the sort of thing that made you shiver and turn to another page. He took the collar and fitted it round Korsan. She was right.

"One day," she said, "one day when you have another collar, you can bring this one back. So tell your mother that it is a loan, from one animal lover to another." Put like that it sounded all right.

"That horse could do with feeding up," grumbled the porter. "Seems like a waste of good ointment. Hasn't anyone got grass that wants cutting round your way?"

"That's a good idea," said Mehmet, and the man almost smiled at them.

The road back seemed shorter, and they agreed that if there were more people like the lady vet around, life might be easier for people like them.

"That's why I'm going back to school," said Mehmet. "I figure it's knowing things that makes people like that."

"My parents never sent me to school. None of us went, and we don't know anything," Muhlis remarked unexpectedly.

"How did your brother learn to write, then?"

"They taught him in the army. I expect I'll learn when I go . . . but what'll happen to Yıldız then?"

"Your brother'll be back then, won't he? How old are you anyway?"

"My brother says I'm twelve or thirteen. It's like I said, we don't know anything. None of us do. There were thirteen children in our family, and Ramazan and I were the last two boys, I suppose."

"Don't you know?"

"No, and I don't care either. They may have had more children after us. I've never been back to find out and I never will."

"You mean . . . you ran away?" Mehmet had seen newspaper stories about that, too. People ran away in his village, but only for a few days, to keep out of sight while some argument settled down. Young people ran away to get married — Elif and Osman had — and after all the shouting everybody forgot about it. But running away and never going back — that was different. It must be a bit like dying.

"You mean you're on your own? You live on your own here?"

"Yes. Well, no. I've got Yıldız, haven't I? She's better company than my family ever was. She's always pleased to see me."

"Your family *must* have been pleased to see you." It was something that Mehmet didn't understand. Even horrid, horrid parents like Yusuf Amca and Fatma Teyze, the kind of parents you wouldn't have wanted — even they were liked by their own children, or so it seemed.

"Not my parents. My mother said that we children were her punishment. She said that we were nothing but mouths to feed, nothing but a problem. My parents weren't sad when some of the babies died. Oh, they didn't mind the girls so much. Father got money when he married them off. They married my sister off when she was twelve." The two friends walked on in silence. They were both more or less twelve. Perhaps it was different for girls, but surely not that different. Ayşe was sixteen, he knew, and for all her grown-up ways, she still played jump rope in the evening with her friends. The girls swung somebody's washing line and leaped and leaped with their brightly colored dresses flying. He had the feeling that Elif, craning her neck from the empty window to watch, wanted to be out there, too; she often was if Osman was not at home. So it couldn't be that different for girls. But now that he thought about it, Ayşe hadn't skipped rope since she had started work in the city. It looked as though working made you more grown up than marrying. School certainly didn't make you grown up. He thought of Hayri;

he was the sort of person one couldn't imagine outside school, grown up and married. People in the village had said there was something magic about him and whispered prayers over him and spat to keep away the devil. They had all taken care of Hayri, who might always be a child. But not Muhlis; it was hard to think of him ever being somebody's little child.

"What happened to her then, this sister?"

"I dunno, not properly. The fellow — an old fellow he was and a friend of our father's — took her off, and we never heard from her again. Well, not exactly. Neighbors said she tried to run away several times, and I don't blame her." He laughed bitterly. "It must be in the family. We ran off just after that."

"What did she do, then, all on her own?"

Muhlis didn't answer but went on hurriedly with his own story. "We didn't plan it. My brother had had a beating from Father, a real bad one that made his back bleed. We thought we'd just keep out of the way for a few days. We climbed into the back of an empty truck to get out of the sun. You know how the sun burns on top of cuts. It makes your back so stiff you can't move. Well, when the truck started up, we said, 'Why not?' So we stayed put."

"Didn't anybody find you?"

"Yes, the driver, but he didn't mind. We weren't doing any harm, were we?"

Mehmet was silent. He wondered whether he would have run off or whether he would have stayed on to be beaten again.

"He was all right, that driver. He shared his food with

57

us, bread and onions and cheese. Do you know, he showed us a photo of his son, a little kid all dressed up in his best clothes, and he said he'd never beaten him. That's what made me think that things could be different. Ramazan had always said that, but I didn't believe him till that man showed me that photo. He took Ramazan into a pharmacy and got something for his back. I'd never been in a pharmacy; we didn't have one in our village, and I'd never seen medicine. We didn't have anything in our village. If you were sick, your family either decided that you were too ill to be carried into town and would die on the way and then it wouldn't be worth the trouble, or they decided that you were only slightly ill and could get better without the help of a doctor. I tell you, there weren't many old people in our village. No, that driver was all right; he was like the vet. Ramazan says that people start off all right but some of them go rotten, like rotten potatoes, and you've got to recognize the stink. He says he can read a person's face better than he could ever read what might be written in a book."

Muhlis laughed cheerfully.

"Ramazan said he knew what your aunt was like with his eyes shut. He'd had his eye on that old carpet of hers for weeks. He got to know her by buying old clothes from her at twice their value and acting like he was stupid. When he'd got enough money together he bought a new carpet — that bright red one — and took it round all wrapped up on his pushcart. It was several days before a *bayram*, and he said it was for a neighbor of hers. He let your aunt touch a corner of it: those machine-made carpets do feel nice to touch when they're new. I can hear him now: 'Fatma *Hanım*, I'm sorry to disappoint you. It's only somebody like yourself, who knows about quality, who can appreciate a fine carpet like this, but I'm afraid it's promised to Nermin Hanım and she's not in today. I'll have to bring it back tomorrow.' And he did because he knew the neighbor had gone away on a *bayram* visit. He brought that carpet back for four days in a row, and he could see your aunt wanting it more and more. It was pretty even though it was so cheap.

"He waited until the end of the week when she was doing her big cleaning just before the *bayram* and had all her furniture out in the garden. Then he came by with his pushcart, really slowly, and she called him over. Would he just let her try the carpet for size, in her guest room? He did, of course, and then he helped her put all the furniture back on top of it, 'just to see how it looked.' She thought it looked really nice, and you could see how much she wanted it. She kept glancing at her watch; she had to get it all finished before your uncle came back. Then Ramazan said, 'Look here, Fatma Hanım, since you're somebody I respect like a mother, I can't take your money — I wouldn't feel happy about it. I'll take your old carpet away in exchange,' and he did."

"Why did he do that?"

"Because the old carpet was valuable! He'd been into the city and looked at all the prices of carpets in the shops. It was what you call an antique. Rich people pay a lot of money for things that are really old. We went straight into town and sold that carpet for a lot of money. It was

Ramazan's first big money. It was because of that he could get Yıldız and the cart from the coal man." He clapped Mehmet on the shoulder and laughed. "Hey, don't feel so bad about your aunt — we've got a lot to thank her for!"

But it was not his aunt that made Mehmet feel so uneasy; it was Hakan. If Ramazan was right and you could read people, then Mehmet read something about sleek, shiny Hakan that was dangerous.

⋅⋅{ 5 }⋅⋅

OSMAN DAYI had found a job — a real job. Even he could not quite believe it. Elif had read about it in the newspaper and insisted that he try for it. He'd sat an examination with hundreds of others. Nobody believed he'd get the job; some of the men at the examination had university degrees. Yusuf Amca declared it impossible: you had to know the right person. But he got the job. Then Yusuf said that there must have been a mix-up over the names, but it didn't really matter. Osman had the letter in his hand and could start work as a porter in a bank. He was to take tea to people, show strangers where they had to go, and carry around papers — important papers. He'd get a free suit and a pair of shoes now and a winter coat and another pair of shoes later. Even Yusuf Amca could not spoil Elif and Osman's excitement, nor could the very small salary. When you have had nothing, a small amount of money makes you feel very rich.

"I told you," said Mehmet's father. "It's making a start that is important. A bright boy like you, there'll be no stopping you." He himself had begun to look old lately. He said less and less about his work in his brother's workshop. They knew he was looking out for something else, but so were thousands of others, and many were younger and stronger than him.

Ayşe went to work with him most mornings, but she didn't say much about her work either. Each week she divided her money into three and sat by the window and sewed. She sewed garlands of flowers until she could see no more. Mehmet's mother, grandmother, and Elif were busy around the house and with the younger children and with their new neighbors. The other women were very friendly at first. It was now high summer. The women gathered together each afternoon in the shade of some building. They knitted and sewed and watched the children and gossiped. Sometimes Fatma Teyze joined them. Someone usually fetched a cushion for her. Mehmet wasn't sure whether it was because she was so fat or so rich; whichever it was, she was treated with respect. Mehmet, as a boy, was too old for such gatherings; he did not want to join them anyway. Hakan, though older, was encouraged to stay, because everyone knew that he was delicate. He rarely joined in the conversation, but he listened and watched the women and nibbled cookies. One of the women, trying to be pleasant to him because he was Fatma Hanım's son, asked him a few questions.

"Are you pleased to have your cousin Mehmet here now?"

"Oh, naturally," said Hakan, who was always polite.

"We are all very glad that he has come, he and his family." The ladies nodded and stitched. There was no denying it: Fatma Hanım certainly had polite children. It was very hot. They wiped their faces with their scarves, and one fanned herself with the back of a packet of cookies.

"I'd like to spend more time with Mehmet, if only he wasn't working," continued Hakan, making himself look very, very lonely and left behind.

"But he isn't working," protested Mehmet's mother in surprise. Then she smiled with pleasure and pride as she informed her neighbors, "Mehmet will be going on to secondary school in the autumn, God willing."

"I thought he must be working, since he never seems to be around now," said Hakan. "I thought he must be getting quite good money somewhere, since he was able to buy that collar. . . ."

"What collar?" The ladies paused in their stitching.

"The dog collar, Korsan's new collar," explained Hakan. "Mehmet must have paid a lot of money for it. It's one of those real leather ones with brass studs."

"Oh, no," said Mehmet's mother. "He didn't buy it."

"Oh, I see," breathed Hakan. "He just . . . found it . . . did he?"

The ladies raised their eyes from their complicated patterns and watched Mehmet's mother curiously as she tried to explain the story of how Mehmet had been lent the dog collar by a lady vet. It was a complicated tale, and she didn't tell it well, and the little group became silent in the hot afternoon. The ladies clearly wondered why Mehmet, who did not seem special at all, should have had such a piece of luck. The children on Happy Hill were not lent things; oh, sometimes they were given things, but only when nobody else wanted them. The neighbors did not really feel suspicious, but all the same. . . . The ladies leaned back and enjoyed the shiver of suspicion that Hakan had aroused in them.

"Well, well," said Fatma Teyze. She said it in a very odd way. Then she continued, very loudly and firmly, as though she wished to hurry them all on to some other topic of conversation, "Well, well! Children will be children. There's no knowing what they get up to, is there? Yusuf Bey and I always say, 'The rod comes straight from Heaven.' " She rewound her wool very firmly and stitched fiercely, without once glancing at her sister-in-law. When the group broke up and the ladies headed back to their own homes, they all went with an uncomfortable feeling that maybe there was something not quite right about this family up from the country. It did seem odd that such an ordinary boy should have such luck.

Then Yusuf Amca lost his shoes. He had left them outside the front door, and they had vanished. This often happened in the shantytown. Washing left on the line, shoes left outside the door, a bag of vegetables left unguarded at the market: you had to keep your eyes on things. Everybody in the shantytown knew that. Yusuf Bey, however, was different. Number 1 was, after all, the nicest house on Steep Way, and it would have to be a brave thief who would walk up and snatch those shoes in broad daylight. Yusuf Bey made a great fuss. They were new shoes made of soft white leather and they did not squeeze his corns. There was a general search.

"I've told you all, time and time again, not to leave

shoes outside the house!" he roared. His family scurried around searching and did not dare remind him that he had left the shoes outside himself. When Yusuf Bey lost his temper completely, he reached for his stick. They asked the neighbors, but nobody had seen a pair of white leather shoes. Hakan was unusually energetic and helpful.

"I'll go round and look for you, father," he said.

"Now, don't you bother, dear," said his mother. "You know you'll only get overheated running up and down the street in this heat."

"Oh, I won't go far. I'll only go up and ask Muhlis and Mehmet," said Hakan pleasantly.

"You'll do no such thing!" cried his mother. "You're not to go near that filthy Muhlis. You might catch something."

"I've only got to ask them."

"No, dear, someone else can do that."

"Why can't Hakan?" said Yusuf Bey sourly. If he didn't find those shoes, his feet would kill him. They always swelled in this heat.

"I'll go," said Hakan. "I won't run, and anyway, Mehmet and Muhlis are sure to know about the shoes. . . ."

"Why?" demanded his parents in one breath.

"Well," said Hakan, not looking at them, "that's what Muhlis deals in, isn't it? And everybody knows that Mehmet is helping him and they may have . . . well, I mean . . . thought that you did not need the shoes . . . or something like that." He smiled the bright smile of a liar.

"So that's what our young relative is up to, is it?" said Yusuf Bey even more sourly, and he remembered the affair of the red carpet with renewed anger.

Somehow or other everybody in the neighborhood knew that Yusuf Bey had had to ask his very own nephew about the lost shoes. It was shocking, and this was the family whom Yusuf Bey was looking after, too. People repeated the proverb about the crow: "If you rear a crow, then one day it will peck out your eye." Rumors, as fat and swollen as the big blue-bellied flies that droned over the rubbish piles, began to circulate in Happy Hill. Nobody said anything straight out, but Mehmet's mother no longer enjoyed her afternoons. She secretly felt that people were suspicious of her and her family, but she did not speak of this.

Mehmet was unaware of the rumors. He was increasingly busy with Muhlis and Yıldız. The horse's leg had healed. She was no longer lame and now pulled the cart with ease. Muhlis wanted her to look perfect before his brother's return but it was clear that she needed more food. She needed fresh grass. He remembered the advice of the scowling porter at the Veterinary Clinic and reminded Mehmet about it. Why shouldn't they try and get work cutting grass and then keep the cut grass for Yıldız? Mehmet liked the idea. He knew more about plants and gardens than he did about old clothes and scrap iron. He knew how to scythe, too. They decided to ask for work at some of the big houses they had seen on their way into town. There were very large houses on the hill by the Meteorological Station. Mehmet's father agreed to lend them his tools: he had brought them from the village ready for the day when he could dig his own garden. Mehmet's mother was not so enthusiastic. She had seen the neighbors standing in groups and watching her son as he passed by with Muhlis. She wished he'd found a better friend. Hakan might be a dull boy, but he had nice manners.

One fine morning, Mehmet and Muhlis tied Korsan to the back of the cart, and Muhlis clicked his tongue, and Yıldız pulled with a will. A haze hung over the great city — a haze of smoke and dust. Muhlis said it was as though the reddish earth had been powdered up and painted across the sky. The road ahead shimmered. Already patches of tar were melting. It was going to be very hot, so they made some hats out of folded newspapers. Korsan couldn't keep his hat on because it kept slipping over his big wrinkled forehead. His tail drooped, and he panted; his thick coat was not suited to the high, hot Ankara Plain.

They asked for work at many houses. Most of the people turned them down right away. Others said truthfully that they did not have much grass to cut. In Ankara, you have to be very rich to grow grass that is long enough to cut. Finally, one elderly lady paused on her white and yellow marble steps and looked at them again. She asked if Korsan was *really* safe and if they *really* knew how to scythe grass. She must have been very old, for her hands were freckled and knotted with veins. Her hair, which was not hidden under a scarf, was white — absolutely white — and it was wound up on top of her head as though she didn't mind people looking at it. Her face was pale, and her skin was soft and clear and had little lines all over it. She didn't have the deep, brown wrinkles of the old people that Mehmet knew. She looked as though

67

she had rarely been in the sun. She led them round the house into a garden that was much bigger than either of them had expected. It had a high stone wall all around it, and in the center was a very green lawn. Mehmet cut a fine, straight swath down the edge, and the grass was as soft to touch as the fleece of a newly born lamb. She agreed to let them work in her garden and told them that her name was Zekiye Hanım.

It was a beautiful garden. On the other side of the wall, where Yıldız waited patiently under a stunted tree, the struggling grasses were drying in the sun and the thistles were losing their color and shriveling into hard, tearing points. Here in the garden it was cooler, and the air itself was shady and moist. The tall green grass fell in rippling waves before the skimming blade. Mehmet went in front, and Muhlis followed behind, raking the cut grass into careful piles. When they had finished, Zekiye Hanım brought them iced water in a glass jug and then poured it, with the ice tinkling down, into two glasses that had flowers engraved on them. Mehmet, feeling sweaty and dirty, was almost afraid to touch his. Zekiye Hanım said that if they cared to weed and dig over the rest of the garden, she would give them lunch and pay them for their work.

"See?" said Muhlis. "Some people are all right, even women. You can see it in her face, that she is open and not all hidden."

They wondered if Zekiye Hanım lived alone in this great house. No sound came from it. Indeed it was very quiet inside the walled garden. The noise from the city, like the roar from some animal that will not lie still, was

68

held back by the walls and reached them only as a whispering moan. The only sound was that of metal on earth, as Muhlis thrust the spade deeply into the damp, yielding soil. They scarcely spoke, not wanting to spoil this stillness.

The fruit trees at the end of the garden had grown big and ungainly, and the fruit forming along the branches was small and diseased. It must have been years since the trees were sprayed. Perfect though the garden appeared at first glance, there was a lot of work that needed doing, and Mehmet was glad. Once, when they were sweeping the paths around the house, they looked into a room and saw Zekiye Hanım sitting at a desk, reading. It was shadowy in the room, but they could see the shine of old silver on the little tables, and beside her gleamed a bowl of roses. Along one wall were books — hundreds and hundreds of books. They stepped back and did not look in again. When they had finished, they sat on the marble steps, waiting for Zekiye Hanım to come out, and they looked at the garden with pride. The roses bloomed and glowed like jewels, and their scent mingled with the scent of the newly cut grass.

"That's what Ramazan says he wants, a house of his own with roses in the garden. I'd like a fountain — it doesn't have to be a big one, but just enough so that the wind would blow a bit of spray on your face on a hot evening," said Muhlis.

Zekiye Hanım thanked them and paid them fairly and said that they might come back again in two weeks, when the grass would be long enough to scythe again. They went away slowly and almost unwillingly; Mehmet could

69

have worked in that garden forever even without being paid. He wondered if the old lady ever went beyond those high walls. If he lived there, he wouldn't leave to come out here on the dusty road, where the sun was so bright that you couldn't see without screwing up your eyes. If you lived in that house, you could forget about the world outside.

The road back to Şentepe rose slowly and steadily; they walked to save Yıldız. Ten minutes from home Mehmet heard someone calling his name. It was Hakan. He was sitting on an upturned box outside a grocer's shop, draining a bottle of cola.

"Mehmet, Muhlis, come over here," he called. He tipped the bottle up and noisily sucked out the last drops.

"Well?" They stopped but didn't go over.

"You still in the old clothes business?" he asked, looking at the bags of grass on the cart.

"It depends. . . ." Muhlis was cautious.

"What do you mean, 'it depends'? You always used to buy clothes from me."

"It still depends. . . ."

"Well, if you are, I've got some things for you. And if you're not interested, there are plenty of other gypsies, so please yourself." He took another bottle from the crate. Mehmet made a motion to lead Yıldız on, but Muhlis paused.

"If I am, shall I come to your house?"

"Are you joking?"

"Will you come to me?"

"I might."

"When?"

70

"I'll find you," said Hakan, and he took a handful of sunflower seeds from his pocket and began to crack them very fast between his teeth. He spat the husks into the dust at their feet.

"Suit yourself," Muhlis grinned, then led the cart so close to Hakan that he had to draw in his new summer sports shoes in haste.

"I didn't know that Hakan sold things to you. I thought you just did the one deal, the carpet deal with his mother."

"Where do you think your cousin gets all his money?"

"From his mother?" As he suggested it, Mehmet couldn't really imagine his aunt being so generous, even to Hakan.

"No, he sells things to me, clothes and things."

"Doesn't his mother notice? My mother would." It was true. He had lost a handkerchief once, and she had noticed even that.

"I dunno," said Muhlis and shrugged. "That's his problem, not mine."

It made Mehmet uneasy: that was one of the differences about life here. In the village, you knew more or less what would happen. Here, it was as though you were always waiting for something you did not know about. It made him scared. Hakan scared him. He wished he was like Muhlis, who lolled against the sacks on the cart, his long legs dangling and his crazy, triangular hat stuck back on his head. He didn't look scared. They passed a man who sold beads and plastic jewelry and glass diamonds. There was a crowd of women and girls turning over the sparkling, plastic gold. Mehmet elbowed his way through

71

and bought two blue glass beads in the shape of eyes, one for Korsan and one for Yıldız, to keep them safe from the Evil Eye.

It grew hotter and hotter as the days went by. Once it seemed that it must rain: the air felt heavy and pressed down on you, and the sweat ran and soaked your clothes and didn't dry. Mehmet walked out onto the plains with Muhlis. They squatted down and watched the lightning cracking the sky over the distant mountains, but no rain fell. Some houses, like Yusuf's, had water piped into them. But many families, like Mehmet's, had to collect their water from a public tap. Now the supply of water was cut, not only for hours on end, but for days on end. People had to line up to fill their water containers. In the heat and worry that the water would be cut off before your turn came, there were ugly quarrels and fights. Elif, waiting in the hot sun for several hours, had fainted and come home white and trembling with the water container unfilled. After that it became Mehmet's task to wait in the water line. Sometimes Hakan would pass by, licking an ice or drinking a fruit juice, and Mehmet imagined the eyes of the people in the line, comparing him with his cousin. Then one day, he heard some women behind him gossiping.

"Who said that?" The speaker squeaked with outrage.

"Fatma Hanım did. She told me herself. Her *own* nephew, too. . . ." Mehmet longed to turn around but knew that if he did, he wouldn't have dared to say anything to these women.

"She's very ashamed. Poor Fatma Hanım! She's a person of very high ideals."

"What's gone?"

"Well, she didn't actually say that anything had gone. I mean, she wouldn't, with them being her husband's relatives, but she said that since they came from the village, her family had to take care that nothing went missing!"

"How wicked! Still, I must say I have my doubts about them. Have you seen their daughter-in-law? All decked out like a village beauty? She's a sharp piece of goods. I've seen her out in the evening playing with the other girls, for all the world to see, just as if she hasn't got a husband at home, if he is her husband. . . ."

Had Elif heard something like this? Maybe it wasn't the heat that had made her faint. Mehmet wished that he could have told someone. He waited in line for five hours and never once turned around. He disliked himself for being a coward. Muhlis would have turned around — or would he? He was never sure if Muhlis cared about anything at all, except for Yıldız. Toward evening a whistling rush of air in the tap told them that the water was coming. He thought about the cool, soft grass in the old lady's garden. Zekiye Hanım had said that she watered it every evening. It felt softer to your feet than any carpet.

Another letter came for Muhlis: his brother Ramazan would be home on leave next month. Muhlis was excited. It was a long time to wait, but it also gave him time to make preparations. Ramazan would want to see things well looked after. Muhlis decided to repaint the cart. He chose green, which, he said, was a lucky color. He painted pictures around the sides. He painted mountains and valleys and shining suns, all linked with whirling, twirling coils of flowers. Then, at the back where it showed, he painted a white house, with white steps and a green, green garden. In the garden he painted a fountain, a fountain gushing out blue and white water, and the water drops made a pattern and flowed away down the sides of the cart into two waterfalls. It was astonishing — and also very beautiful. The children in the shantytown had been warned by their parents to keep away from gypsy Muhlis, but this painting fascinated them. They couldn't stay away. They crept back and watched in admiration as the cart was transformed. Mehmet was amazed. He hadn't thought that somebody who couldn't read or write could do anything like that. When Zekiye Hanım saw it, she admired it very much but said she was not so surprised. She told them that as a girl she had lived in a house by the sea and all the doors of that house had been covered by pictures. They had also been painted by a man who couldn't read or write. She said that as a child she had thought those pictures were the most beautiful things she had seen. They were pictures of the sea, of boats and fish and curling waves on jagged rocks; and there was one of a storm on a dark night, which had given her nightmares as a little girl. Her son and his family went to that house now. They stayed there every year in the summer, and they always asked her to go, too. She never went because she didn't like to leave her house and garden. She said that her garden would dry up in two or three days — dry up and die.

"Is there always water?" asked Mehmet.

"Yes, we always have water. My son has put in a huge water tank and a very strong pump. I've never run out of water yet. I can leave it spraying on the roses all night. How else do you imagine they bloom so well?"

She was right, of course. Yes, she watered her garden, and she read her books behind her high wall. She explained that books were like plants, too: if you did not read them and take an interest in them, they cracked and went yellow and were spoiled by the dust.

Mehmet listened to her, and then he told her about his friend Hayri, who loved books so much. He told her how Hayri had had books sent all the way from Istanbul and that he was studying here in Ankara in a famous school. Zekiye Hanım said that she would like to meet him and that her grandchildren went to a famous school, too. They agreed that it would have been a shame for her to go away and neglect either the garden or her books. She waved good-bye to them over the wall and promised to water the garden extra well so that there would be plenty of grass to cut for Yıldız.

Mehmet had never been into Muhlis's house. He had always waited for him on a stony mound outside. He only knew that it looked very little. Having finished the painting, Muhlis had decided to improve the house by buying a stove. Now he wanted to make a hole in the roof to fit in the stovepipes and erect some sort of chimney. It was to be finished before Ramazan's arrival, and Mehmet was going to help.

When Mehmet knocked on the door early in the morning there was no reply and he guessed that Muhlis must have gone to see Yıldız. Perhaps he could make a start: he knew from experience that putting up a stove always took much longer than expected. He pushed at the door. It swung wildly. The top corner dipped towards the inside of the house, and the bottom corner swung out and hit Mehmet on the shin. Then it fell down to the ground with a terrible clatter and a great cloud of dust rose up from inside the house. Korsan leaped back in alarm. Mehmet rubbed his shin and climbed cautiously over the door: it wasn't really a house at all.

Ramazan and Muhlis, or somebody else, had filled in the tiny space between two other houses. There was a back wall made of gray blocks, one piled on top of the other and smeared with mud. There was a lower front wall with a door-size gap left in it. The door that he had knocked down had just been propped up. The back wall was higher than the front, and several big pieces of wood sloped down from the higher to the lower wall. Plastic sheeting and other things, too, had been stretched over these beams to make a roof, but it was too dark inside to see clearly. At the back of the room, there was an iron bedstead with a thin, dirty mattress and a few ragged blankets. In a corner was a pile of boxes and bags. There were some plastic containers of water in another corner, and beside them, struggling blades of grass grew out of the earth floor, where the water must have dribbled and trickled down. The grass bent, yellow and weak, toward the light that came in through the doorway. There was nothing else in the house, except for Yıldız's harness, which stood against the wall.

Mehmet raised the door hurriedly and stood it up again

outside. It had fallen down on the stove and pipes, but there did not seem to be any damage. Mehmet was stacking the pipes back when Muhlis arrived. If he noticed anything, he did not say, but began filling the kettle from the water container. Mehmet saw a few drops going down toward the grass — just enough to keep them from dying but not enough to make them grow strongly. He had to get out. The dust and closeness of that small, dark space stifled him. There it was again: the unexpectedness of life here in the shantytown. It crept up on you when your back was turned and when you least expected it. It startled you so much that you breathed in great mouthfuls of dirt and dust. Muhlis did not seem to notice.

"It'll be really nice when I get the stove in," Muhlis said.

"I'll see if the grocer has got any fresh bread." Mehmet jumped up and ran out. He bought warm bread to eat with the tea, but he wished he could have bought honey or jam or salty white cheese to have cleared the dust out of their throats.

Muhlis wanted the stove at the back of the house because he always sat on the bed in the winter. Mehmet agreed: the stove would burn better with a longer pipe. They had to work from inside for clearly the roof would not stand the weight of somebody standing on it. It was hard, awkward work. Last winter, in an effort to keep out the cold, Muhlis had stuffed in layer upon layer of plastic bags and old rags and smeared them with mud and plaster. Now, as they worked, trying to cut and pick a hole upward, the roof creaked and wobbled and showers of dirt and plaster fell down on them.

"Your stuff'll get messed up." Mehmet nodded at the boxes and bags in which Muhlis kept the things that he sold.

"It's only old rubbish." Muhlis didn't seem to care.

"It's a shame. Look, I'll move it outside and we can dust it and bring it in when we're finished." Mehmet carried the boxes and bags outside, and then they worked on. At last they got through and could shove the pipe into the hole in the roof. It was Mehmet who thought of the sheet of metal. At home they had used one to prevent the hot ash from falling onto the floor. Here they needed it to prevent the metal legs of the stove from sinking into the earth floor.

"Haven't you got anything like that among your stuff?" He knew that Muhlis collected scrap metal.

"Go and look in that big box; there are shoes and leather things on top, but I think I had some sheets of something at the bottom." He was right. Mehmet tipped out the shoes and found several flattened-out oil cans. He hammered them neatly over a wooden board. They stood the stove on it and fitted the long pipe into the neck of the stove. It looked good.

"Shall we try it?" Muhlis nodded, and they put in some papers and sticks and rags from the roof. Muhlis lit a match. They watched excitedly. It smoked a bit, and Muhlis cursed.

"It always does, when the pipes are cold." Mehmet gathered up more odds and ends and fed them in. Now it roared up.

"You've no idea how cold it was last winter. I thought Yıldız would freeze," said Muhlis.

78

"You'll have to be careful she doesn't scorch her tail now." Mehmet wondered how on earth they had managed in there last winter — he and the horse.

"Look, let's see it from the outside." Mehmet wanted to get out into the fresh air. He walked backward, peering up at the roof to see if the smoke was rising in a straight line, and he stumbled over a pair of legs. It was Hakan, lounging on one of the boxes and stuffing a peach into his mouth.

"I told you I'd find you," he said.

"Well?" Muhlis came out and leaned against the wall.

"Like I said, are you interested?"

"Depends. . . ."

"Take a look." He pointed to a red plastic bag. Muhlis looked through an assortment of women's and children's clothes.

"How much?"

"Ten thousand." Hakan took another peach from his pocket and sucked out some of the soft, scented flesh.

"I don't want it." Muhlis went back inside. Hakan stood up.

"Eight — it's all new, really new." Muhlis came out slowly and touched the bag with his foot.

"It's not worth more than five to me."

"What do you mean? That blouse there is worth five!"

"Go and sell it yourself then."

"Look, I'm busy. I'll take seven." Muhlis reached inside his shirt and brought out a bundle of bills. He counted out five and then added another and held it out.

"You're nothing but a thieving gypsy," said Hakan, and he flung his half-eaten peach angrily away.

"That's right." Muhlis grinned. "Six — take it or leave it." Hakan snatched the bills and stuffed them in his back pocket. Muhlis laughed loudly.

Hakan turned away and then hissed back to them, "You should be more careful. You shouldn't leave your stuff out here where everyone can see it. I mean, everyone knows that my father lost his shoes and just look: there they are, among your stuff!"

"You sold them to me," said Muhlis.

"Prove it. Go on, prove it." Haken worked the squashed peach down into the dust.

Two days later Muhlis took Mehmet into Ankara by *dolmuş,* and they climbed the narrow, winding streets into the old part of the town. There, in the back room of a shop that had clothes hanging out over the pavement, they sold some of the things that Hakan had brought. A fat old hag with her white hair dyed a brilliant orange argued and bargained over every *lira*, but it was a game that Muhlis knew how to play. He came away with a big wad of bills, some of which he hid deep inside his clothes and the rest he put in his jacket pocket. He said he'd come back in a few days with a selection of men's shoes and clothes.

Then, instead of returning down the hill, Muhlis led Mehmet farther up it. Here the streets were even narrower, and the balconies of the houses overhung them so that the sun broke through only now and then. Ragged children sat on flights of broken steps and watched them pass in silence. Sometimes when you paused, the sound of women's voices floated through the shuttered windows. It was quiet but not peaceful, and you found yourself turning around as though somebody might be following you quietly and too closely. Muhlis stopped at a dark door and knocked. Mehmet sensed a movement above him and felt that someone had looked down on them. They heard footsteps and perhaps the creaking of a stair. The door opened just a little. He did not see the face; he only saw a woman's slim, white wrist reach out and small, fine fingers grasp the bills that Muhlis held out through the barely open door. The fingernails were bright red, as perfect and clear as drops of fresh blood.

The door shut and Muhlis said loudly, "Come on, I've got something to show you." Mehmet could only follow, knowing that he was a stranger here and did not yet recognize the landscape.

They were somewhere very high.

"It's a castle," said Muhlis, and he was right. They were on the parapet of the old Ankara Castle. Standing there, in the old castle gardens, were cannons and huge stone cannonballs and narrow-necked jars the size of a man. There were statues — bits of people carved in stone, maybe not finished, maybe finished and later smashed. Mehmet thought again of Hayri and how he would have known about these things. Muhlis had obviously been here often. He called to Mehmet to look at this and that, as though he and the castle were old friends. Mehmet, however, was drawn back to the parapet and the huge city spreading out below them. He had to know where they were in this seemingly endless city.

"Over there — see that hill, with the quarry on the left?" Mehmet could see it now, a towering cut of gray rock.

"There, see those houses with the sloping roofs?"

"Yes." He could even make those out when he looked carefully.

"That's what they call the Meteorological Station. Zekiye Hanım's house is up there."

"Which one is it?"

"You can't see *that* well! But hang on — might it be that one, where it's all green?"

"And us?" Mehmet shaded his eyes and looked even farther, and now he could see hills and hills and more hills all covered with the tiny houses of the shantytown. They ringed the city for as far as he could see. Once, back in the village, he and Hayri had come upon a great flock of little brown birds that had settled, twittering and rustling, on every hedge and tree. Hayri had said that they were traveling south to seek a warmer home before the coming winter.

"You can't see us, not at all," he said, disappointed.

"Of course you can't see Happy Hill," said Muhlis, laughing at him.

·{ 6 }·

I T WAS HOTTER still. Mehmet's mother had
nailed sheets over most of the empty windows,
but it was impossible to keep the house cool. And by day
they were plagued by flies. They settled on your food as
you raised the spoon to your mouth and they crawled
along your eyelids and round your nose. With the coming
of darkness, the mosquitoes rose up in great, humming
clouds. Even when you thought you had covered yourself completely with a sheet, the high whine of yet another disturbed your sleep. The children scratched and
scratched until they bled.

One night it was extra bad. The older people said that
there was a storm coming: flies always came indoors
before a storm. Once Mehmet awoke, and he sat with his
grandfather and they watched the lightning forking in the
distance, but no rain fell. In the morning Mehmet was to
go to Zekiye Hanım's house, so he was glad to get up
early. He sharpened the scythe, then hurried out on hear-

83

ing the clink of Yıldız's hooves. It was oppressively hot. A sudden scurry blew the dust up into their faces. The wind was warm, and the grit grated between their teeth. They urged Yıldız on, eager to reach the cooling green of the walled garden.

They set to work, Mehmet scything the grass and Muhlis weeding between the rosebushes. It was too hot to talk, and the garden was quieter than they had ever known it. Not a leaf stirred. The cut grass shriveled as soon as it fell. Zekiye Hanım, who liked to talk and help a little, sat on the balcony and fanned herself and looked out to the distant mountains. She said that a storm must be coming. At lunchtime they knocked on the door and fetched their tray of bread, olives, and fruit, then searched for some shade. Today even the shadows were warm. They soaked their heads and shirts from the hose, trying to refresh themselves, but their clothes felt heavy and chill instead. They raked the grass into a pile, then began sweeping and washing the paths and steps.

Suddenly Zekiye Hanım banged on the window and shook her head, as if she didn't want them to continue working. She pointed repeatedly to something in the distance, and when they did not understand, she came back onto the balcony.

"Your work will be wasted. Look over there — don't you see the storm coming?"

"I don't see any clouds," said Mehmet, "really I don't. Let us tidy up for you."

"Some storms come without clouds. If you know the signs you can tell. Look!"

"I can't see anything," said Mehmet. "It looks to me like the sun is shining on the mountains."

"Look more carefully."

"I can see a brightness, and the mountains have a dark line around them." Then he shivered as a sharp, twirling wind went over the garden and up the street. They heard windows bang and the scratch of dry papers blown along the base of the wall. He shivered again, and Korsan ran up to him with his tail between his legs and whined.

"Now," insisted Zekiye Hanım, "look again. I've known it was coming for a long time, though I hoped that it would not."

"Did you see that?" called Muhlis. The light behind the mountains — a strange greenish yellow light — became brighter, and there, far beyond the other side of the great city, were three cones of darkness, which looked as though a great hand had scribbled them in the sky. As they watched, the cones grew in size.

"Is it smoke?" Mehmet wondered if something very big was burning.

"No, it's the wind," said Zekiye Hanım.

"But you can't see the wind."

"It's the dirt and dust caught up in the wind. In about half an hour it will be here. It'll be a very strong wind."

"Strong enough to blow things down?" Mehmet thought anxiously of his family in that half-finished building. Another gust rustled the leaves in the garden.

"It'll be strong enough to blow a few roofs off. Now, do you still want to help me?" They nodded. "Then take your shoes off and come indoors quickly and help me fasten down all the shutters and windows before that wind reaches us." They dropped their tools hastily and entered the house for the first time.

Mehmet had seen a few films on neighbors' televisions, so he knew that people in foreign lands lived like this — with bathrooms and polished wooden floors and bedrooms where children slept all alone, except for hundreds of toys. But he had never thought that just one hour's walk away from where he lived there could be houses like this. In the village there had been richer and poorer families, too, but they had all lived in much the same way. Now he had stepped into a different world. He saw a whole shelf of different colored towels in the bathroom and a row of dresses hanging up in a closet, a whole row, like you would see in a shop. Everywhere there were objects — pictures, curtains, rugs — things that were there just because they looked pretty.

The sky was darkening rapidly, and it was not with the coming of evening. The yellow light was deepening and the brightness fading. They quickly started untying the cushions from the white chairs, then began to pack away the furniture on the balcony. Another strong gust thrust against the balcony doors as they tried to shut them. From somewhere up the street they heard glass breaking. Outside, the roses glowed very clearly in the lightless garden.

"You had better get that grass into the bags before the wind really comes," Zekiye Hanım reminded them, and they ran barefoot into the garden. They saw papers swept high up and spinning around in the air, high above the trees. The heap of grass lifted and began to fan upward. Muhlis leaped forward with his arms outstretched to try

86

and save it. He seemed to stumble. He did not cry out. They heard a gasping sound as though the wind had torn his words from him. Then he curled up on the ground with his hands around his foot. He had landed on the curved blade of the scythe that Mehmet had hastily flung down among the grass cuttings. There was blood everywhere.

Mehmet ran over to him. When he lifted Muhlis's hand away from his foot, the wound opened like a crimson mouth. Mehmet grabbed the hose and directed the jet of cold, clear water onto the wound. He was frightened of the blood: if he could wash it away, perhaps the cut was not so bad. But it kept on bleeding. Muhlis lay still, his face the color of dust, one hand pressed to his mouth. Zekiye Hanım begged them again and again to go to a hospital — she would pay, she pleaded. But Muhlis refused: Ramazan was coming home, he said, and he and Yıldız must be there to welcome him. He crawled onto the marble steps while the wind rose higher and higher. With a shaking hand, Mehmet poured iodine into the cut while Muhlis lay back, his cheek pressed against the white- and gold-veined marble. Zekiye Hanım knelt down and bandaged the wound herself, and Mehmet saw that she was crying. The blood quickly soaked through the bandage, and again she begged them to let her go for help, but Muhlis still refused, and leaning on Mehmet, he dragged himself down the steps and onto the cart.

"It was my fault," said Mehmet, picking up the reins. He had thrown down the scythe: everybody knows that you should stand a scythe up. Then at least you can see the blade before it cuts you. He remembered that the scythe was still there, lying like a scorpion in the grass. He jumped down and pulled it clear and hung it up on a branch so that the blade swung to and fro among the rose blossoms. Well, it could just stay there, it and the other tools; they could stay there. Perhaps the coming rain would wash their blades clean.

"It wasn't your fault," Muhlis muttered as Mehmet climbed back onto the cart. "Things like that happen."

"No, Mehmet," said Zekiye Hanım. "It wasn't your fault." She had come hurrying out again with her thin dress flapping in the wind. "It was the storm; I could see it coming. I've seen this storm coming for so long, and yet I could do nothing for you. Now, you must try to protect yourselves." She handed a blanket to Mehmet, who tucked it around Muhlis. Muhlis tried to protest, but the wind got at his words and scattered them.

"If I can do anything, by the name of God, I promise that I will, anytime," Zekiye Hanım cried after them as the wind struck them with greater force. She looked back at the shelter of her garden. Then she set her feet more firmly and stood in the breaking storm, watching as they made their uncertain way before it. Then she stepped back behind the high walls where the wind could do little damage.

It was Yıldız who got them home. Mehmet, with his arm held before his face to protect himself from the flying earth, could barely see; Yıldız was steadier. She only faltered once. A large sheet of red plastic that had been part of a balcony blew down. People screamed and ran out of the way. It crashed down onto the road, its sharp corner biting into the tarmac. The wind flipped it over a couple of times as though it were an autumn leaf. Yıldız threw up her head and stopped. She refused to move. Cars honked behind them. Mehmet jumped down and tried to lead her past, but she would not take one step. The plastic moved a little and slithered along the road. Drivers shouted at them. Mehmet tried to drag Yıldız past again, but she backed suddenly, and he heard Muhlis groan as the unexpected movement rolled him over. Then a great rush of hot wind, which made Mehmet cling to the edge of the cart, lifted the sheet right up. It went crashing and scraping across the road and stopped in just the place where they would have been if Mehmet had been able to drive Yıldız on.

Halfway home the first drops of rain fell — they were big and widely separated. They fell the way overripe plums fall from a tree. One fell on Mehmet's hand, and he saw that it was a faint reddish color. The next moment it started to pour torrentially. In seconds they were soaked. The road through the shantytown was covered by rushing, muddy water. They went even more slowly, for they could no longer see where the deep holes were. People had stopped running for shelter: they were so wet that it made no difference. Then the rain stopped. As suddenly as it had come, it was gone. The children came out smiling and sailed fleets of watermelon rinds in the puddles.

Muhlis's house had not suffered too badly. The high buildings on either side had protected it. The door had blown down, and the rain had come through the roof, but it had sunk away into the earth floor. Mehmet helped his friend to the bed and then took Yıldız out onto the plain. The rain might at least make the grass grow a little.

Mehmet knew he ought to get help for Muhlis and wondered whether his mother could do anything. He went home and found the house in turmoil. The high winds had blown through the empty windows and covered everything in red dust. Then the rain had slashed straight into the house. All their things were wet. There was even water running down the stairs. His mother, drying the floor on her hands and knees, did not stop to greet him. Only Ayşe noticed the blood on his clothes and asked what had happened. He told her that Muhlis had been hurt.

"Shall I come and look?" He nodded gratefully, and they slipped away unnoticed. Ayşe was good with her hands. In a moment she had peeled away the blood-soaked bandages and sent Mehmet out to get disinfectant. She bathed the cut, then rummaged among the boxes until she found a clean shirt. She tore it into strips and bandaged Muhlis's foot again as neatly as if she were a doctor. She made Mehmet light the little stove, and then she went around the cramped house rearranging things. She tidied up, straightening things and fashioning a cushion for Muhlis to rest against and making it all seem less awful. Muhlis followed her movements in silence, and Mehmet wondered if he were thinking about his own sister.

Ayşe found a frying pan and sent Mehmet out for eggs and bread. Then she fried the eggs over the stove and wouldn't go until, laughing and teasing, she had made

Muhlis eat them. Mehmet and Ayşe did not like to leave Muhlis, but they had to since darkness was falling. They set a bottle of water on a box where he could reach it, and then Ayşe turned back. She said she had heard that injured legs should be raised up: she bundled more of the old clothes under the end of the mattress, and Muhlis obediently wriggled down until his foot was propped up. It was surprising. Muhlis never did what other people told him to do.

On their way back to their own house, Mehmet told Ayşe about the gardening and how they had been trying to get everything ready before Muhlis's brother Ramazan came back. He told her how it had all gone wrong and how it had been his fault. He had left the scythe half buried in the grass.

"Anyone could have done that," said Ayşe, laying an arm over his shoulder.

"Why did *he* have to step on it? I mean, he's had enough bad luck. I'd have much rather *I* stepped on it." It was true, and Ayşe was silent because she knew how he felt. Then she nudged him. There, talking to their mother, was Hakan.

"I wish something would happen to *him!*" she murmured. Mehmet looked up at her in astonishment; this was not what you expected from gentle Ayşe. It was the sort of thing that Muhlis said.

"It never seems to, though," she added regretfully. "People like Hakan have skins thicker than water buffaloes." Their mother saw them and ran over.

"Where have you been? Hakan told me that there had

91

been an accident, that he had seen blood on the cart. . . ."
His mother was near tears. Mehmet was silent. He had
not thought of telling, but he hadn't planned to lie either.

"Tell me, quick!" His mother was looking him over for
signs of injury.

"It wasn't me — it was my friend."

"Friend? What friend?"

"You know . . ." He really did not want to tell her
everything.

"He means Muhlis the Thief," said Hakan. "I'm sorry,
Aunty, but everyone else always calls him that — though
I expect you didn't know."

It was more than Mehmet could bear. He couldn't
explain. He couldn't make things right. He couldn't make
it right, ever, but he could knock Hakan down. He felt
giddy with a great surge of power in himself. In front of
his horrified mother and a gathering crowd of curious
neighbors, he knocked Hakan down into the thick, red
mud left by the storm. It wasn't a very good fight. Hakan
did not defend himself. He lay in the mud shrieking for
somebody to save him. Mehmet gave him a few good
thumps and then got up in disgust. His mother started to
help Hakan to his feet, but Ayşe didn't. She said loudly,
"I told you he was like a water buffalo!" Somewhere,
someone laughed.

Mehmet would have been in real trouble in the morning had not his family been troubled by something else.
Elif's little daughter, Filiz, woke up red in the face and
burning with fever. She cried in a weak, squeaky way and

would not eat. When they forced her to, she was sick and cried on feebly. Mehmet's mother, who had seen many ill children, declared her to have caught a cold.

"In this weather?" said Elif. It was a beautiful, fresh sunny day. Then she remembered last night's storm; of course, all the bedding must have been damp. Elif stuck out her chin and listened in silence to Mehmet's mother, who said that the child would soon be better. Getting ill was a part of growing up, she said. Elif looked doubtful but helped them hang all the mattresses and quilts out of the windows. Mehmet caught Ayşe's eye. This was their chance. Mehmet felt like a conspirator as they nodded to each other and left the house unnoticed.

"Is that really what they call him, Muhlis the Thief?" Mehmet asked. He had to know.

"Fatma Teyze does," said Ayşe reluctantly. "But that doesn't mean he shouldn't be looked after, does it?"

"It's not true. I know it's not true." It mattered to Mehmet so much.

"I don't care whether it's true or not," said Ayşe, walking so quickly that he had to run to keep up. "You should help people because they need it, not because they are this or that sort of person." He had never thought about it before, but it sounded right when she said it.

"But what about Hakan?" he asked. "Would you help him?" Ayşe laughed.

"I might. I mean, if a water buffalo really got stuck in the mud, I couldn't leave him to drown." He looked at her admiringly. His grandfather was right: still waters do run deep.

Muhlis was more cheerful. His foot "banged," he said, but when they took off the bandages, it didn't look too bad. The wound was closing in a bumpy dark red line. Ayşe said that since Muhlis had no fever, then it would probably be all right.

"You think I can get down to see Yıldız?" Muhlis whispered.

"Of course you can't — I won't let you." Ayşe sounded just like a mother. "If you walk on that, it will open up again!" Muhlis lay guiltily, as still as a mouse. Mehmet went off to look after Yıldız while Ayşe tidied up. She must have gone through some of the boxes, for when Mehmet came back, she'd spread an old rug on the floor and had put some flowery curtains on the bed. It was all neatly tucked in, and he couldn't believe what a difference it made.

"You don't have to bother," said Muhlis awkwardly. "I mean, I'm used to things; there's nothing that can hurt me." Ayşe was standing in the doorway. Her straight, dark eyebrows were drawn down, and her face was framed by the tumbling, winding silk flowers on the edge of her scarf. She was nice as well as pretty, and Mehmet liked his sister more now than he ever had as a little boy. She shrugged and then left them.

"Have I annoyed her?" asked Muhlis. "I didn't mean it like that. I just meant, well, I don't expect much. I know what people say, not that I care myself, but she doesn't have to come."

"Don't worry," said Mehmet. "Ayşe wouldn't come if she didn't want to. Not now."

Mehmet stayed there most of the day. The other soccer players dropped by in the afternoon. They made themselves tea, sharing the two glasses. Mehmet didn't want to go home. Yesterday's fight might bring a punishment. Hakan was the sort of person whom you could cover with mud and yet it wouldn't stick. The next day he'd be up and about as clean and shiny and treacherous as before. The boys talked about school. It was to reopen in two weeks, after the long summer vacation. Mehmet, they said, must register now. A couple of the boys were already at the secondary school. Another had given up last year because his parents could no longer afford the books. One, a ginger-haired boy whose face was freckled all over, was going to start in the first class like Mehmet. His brother and sister were also still in school; Mehmet could come with them to register.

"Schools don't teach you everything," said Muhlis, screwing up his face as he shifted his leg. "Ramazan says you learn more in the street than you do in school."

"It's true," agreed another. "You can study all you like and there still won't be work at the end of it."

"That's right," said Freckles. "My uncle has finished university — he's an engineer, a real engineer, and do you know what he does?"

"Builds things?"

"No, he's a porter. He carries cases of fruit in the bazaar, and that's when he's lucky!" Mehmet remembered the bent figures of the porters in the bus station, bowed down with the luggage of three and four people on their backs, their fingers in the dust.

"Why are you going to school, then?" he asked Freckles.

"My parents want us to. My parents are teachers, you know." He grinned widely, and all his freckles moved.

"My father says that these days you might as well starve as become a civil servant," said another. "I'm working in a shop. It's better than school, I can tell you." Mehmet thought of Osman. He was a civil servant. Would he starve now? And Hayri — would he end up lugging orange boxes? Mehmet looked around at the faces before him and suddenly, vividly saw Hayri's face so fair and so bright and so full of hope. He remembered their time together in the village school, where Hayri had seemed to do anything and everything but listen to the teacher and yet had always known the right answer. He looked back at his new friends, so steady and serious and hard-working, and he put his hand in his jacket and slowly drew out the piece of paper with Hayri's address on it. He asked them if they knew of it, but he asked casually, unwilling to let them know how much it meant to him. The boys passed it from hand to hand. They said it was on the other side of town — you could get there on a couple of buses. He ought to have gone before; he did not really know why he hadn't. He'd go next week. It would be nice to hear of somebody making a success of something. On this side of town, nothing seemed to be going well. He wondered if they let dogs on the buses; the boys were unsure.

"You can leave him with me," said Freckles eagerly. Korsan was popular, and Freckles would have given a lot to spend a day walking round the shantytown with the big dog at his heels.

In the evening, after work, Ayşe came back. She'd brought some food for Muhlis, and a bottle of medicine.

"I'm not ill!" Muhlis looked alarmed and mistrustful. Ayşe had taken Elif and the baby to the pharmacy and while there had told the lady about Muhlis's accident.

"She said that you ought to have had a shot but that at least this would help."

"It won't do anything to me, will it?" Muhlis had never had medicine before, but he swallowed it bravely. Then Ayşe knelt down on the floor and started to undo the bandage. It had bled a bit more, and the cloth was stuck to the wound.

"See, I told you what would happen if you didn't keep still." She got some water and began to soak the bandage. The boys stood around in a serious circle, remembering accidents they had had and how they had been treated. One showed a deep, brown patch on his shoulder where he had been burned; his mother had poured oil on it, so it hadn't healed.

"My grandmother used to put ash on our cuts," said Freckles. "Even though my parents told her not to, she'd still do it."

"That's wrong," said Ayşe, and they nodded in agreement. She was the undeniable expert. She was rebinding the wound when a movement in the doorway made her look up. For a second, Mehmet thought it was Osman. It was a man, resting his hands on either side of the empty door and stooping down to peer in at them. His face was in shadow. Then Mehmet saw his black boots. He tried to step behind the others. For one fearful moment he thought that his uncle must have made a complaint about

97

him and sent the police to arrest them. Perhaps they were being accused of stealing things. Muhlis did not look at all frightened; instead he was trying to get up from the bed. He made a tottering hop, overturned the basin of water onto Ayşe, and would have fallen had not the big man leaped into the room and caught him up in his arms as though he were a baby.

"It's Ramazan! It's my brother!" cried Muhlis, clinging tightly to the neck of the other. The circle of boys stepped back respectfully before this tall, dark-eyed man of whom they had heard so much. Only Ayşe didn't move. She picked up the basin and brushed the water from her skirts and began to rewind the tumbled bandages and hardly seemed to look at the stranger.

Mehmet left them and walked home slowly, worried now not only about Muhlis's accident but about the fight with Hakan and the punishment it might bring.

As the days passed, Mehmet lived on in suspense. Each evening he expected his aunt or uncle to be waiting for him. Hakan must have told them about the fight. His aunt must have seen Hakan's muddy clothes and bruised face. But if there had been complaints, Mehmet's parents hadn't mentioned it. They were less and less concerned about him every day. Now all their interest was centered around Elif and Filiz.

One evening when Mehmet returned home, he heard raised voices. "I don't care what Yusuf Amca says! We won't stay here!" Elif shouted.

"Yusuf Amca says they'll finish the apartments before

winter. He says that it was an unusual storm and unlucky." Osman's voice was pleading. Mehmet climbed the stairs and looked into the room. His parents were watching the young couple, too shy to interfere and yet not wanting Elif to win. They stared at her with horrified admiration.

"We'll freeze to death! Do you want that? Do you?" Her voice was shrill. "Perhaps you don't care about me, but what about your daughter? Do you want her to die of cold? The pharmacist told me that she had caught a chill from the damp bedding. What sin has she that you make her stay here and get ill again?" It was horribly unfair of Elif, and they knew it, but there was just enough truth in it to keep them quiet and make them watch in fascination.

"You'll do what I say!" yelled Osman in a sudden explosion of useless temper. "If I say we'll move, then we'll move, and if I say we'll stay, we'll stay!" He strode outside, and they heard him kicking his way down the stairs. Elif went back into the little room opposite. A moment later they heard her calling gently and clearly, "Os-man, Os-man!" Then his returning steps echoed and were suddenly swift and light on the stair.

Then one day Elif found her house. She came hurrying to tell them, her eyes shining with victory. Who had said there were no houses to be rented in Şentepe? Nobody bothered to look — that was their trouble. She had found a widow and her daughter who wanted to let one room of their three-roomed house. They were to share the kitchen. The rent was a little more than Elif had expected, but she laughed — Osman had a good job, didn't he? The rain wasn't going to blow in on her again! It would be a real home.

Mehmet was sorry to hear that they were going. He didn't care what people said about Elif, didn't care that they called her a silly, empty-headed girl; she was a beautiful girl, and she had made them all laugh, often with her very silliness. You needed people like that, the way you needed flowers in a garden. No, he was sorry that Osman and Elif were going.

When Fatma Teyze heard, she squashed her lips together and hissed. "If you feed a crow, it'll pick out your eyes!"

Mehmet registered for secondary school and again nobody was very interested. His mother remarked in an irritable way that now they would have to get him a jacket, and just how did he suppose they would find the money? He didn't know whether he was more startled or hurt. They'd joked and teased back in the village about how big your feet were and that you grew faster than the birch trees, but all the same, when the time came to get the new shoes or the longer pair of trousers, his mother had always been more excited and pleased than he had been. But now things had changed. Really, Muhlis didn't know how lucky he was: if you didn't have a family, at least they couldn't upset you.

"I don't have to have a new jacket. I can wear my old one." He could, if it didn't fall apart before then.

"If it's not a jacket, it'll be books, and if it's not books, it'll be pencils. Don't tell me it won't!"

"If you feel like that, I won't go." He wasn't that enthusiastic about it anyway, especially after hearing the boys talk.

"Oh, yes, you will go. After all the trouble you've caused, do you think I'm going to leave you around the streets all day?"

What exactly did she mean? Uncle Yusuf must have complained after all. It wasn't fair. Back in the village even his mother had called Hakan a milk-pudding child and had laughed at him. Now she seemed to see things differently.

"Still," said his mother, "will you promise me to keep out of trouble until school starts?"

"Of course." He wanted to keep out of trouble, but it would have been easier if he had known exactly what she meant by trouble.

"Then," she said, smiling at him, "if you're a good boy, I'll ask your aunt if you can have one of Hakan's old jackets, and perhaps a shirt, too. I'm sure she wouldn't mind."

"And me?" he whispered, but not loudly enough to be heard. How could she be so blind? Couldn't she see how he felt? She looked at him kindly and came over and smoothed down his hair.

"Don't worry, dear. You'll look just as smart as anybody else on the first day of school. It's lucky for you that Hakan is such a fatty. His mother says that he grows out of his clothes while they're still almost new. It's lucky for us." She went on peeling the potatoes as though everything was all right.

Mehmet said he would go and fetch some water. He would do anything to get out of the house. He didn't care if he had to wait in the line all night long. So she really

101

thought he would be happy to wear Hakan's old clothes to school? He'd rather die. Even Muhlis didn't wear them but sold them to a red-haired crone and laughed about it afterward.

It was easy for them to talk about keeping out of trouble. They pushed you into it without noticing that they were doing it. Never had he hated anyone the way he hated Hakan, and now he was expected to wear his old jacket gratefully to school. Well, he wouldn't, and they couldn't make him. And now he hated Hakan even more. He thought suddenly of Hayri. Hayri wouldn't ever get in a mess like this. With Korsan at his heels, Mehmet went slowly down the track to Muhlis's house. For the first time he thought about going back to the village, but how? Anyway, he couldn't go without seeing Hayri first, and who knows, somebody as bright as Hayri might have some good ideas. He decided that at the next opportunity he would go in search of his childhood friend. He had already let too much time pass by.

·{ 7 }··

AT THE LAST moment, when it came to leaving Korsan behind, Mehmet couldn't. Korsan had as much right to see Hayri as he did. Freckles was disappointed; he had even bought a bone for the dog.

"You promised," he said accusingly.

"I know," agreed Mehmet, "but think how he'd feel if he could smell Hayri's smell on me when I got back. He'd think I'd tricked him." They both looked at the dog. It did seem like a mean thing to do. So Freckles went off to play soccer, and Mehmet went to the *dolmuş* stop. This was his second time into town, but on his own it felt like a trip to the other side of the world. What must it be like, then, to go to America? That was about the farthest you could go, and that was where the teacher had said Hayri should go.

"You'll see — give him this chance and there will be no stopping him. He can study in America and be a great scientist." Those were the teacher's words. Hayri, who knew the names of all the Indian tribes in America, had said one day, when they were lying in the grass and eating cherries shaken down from a neighbor's tree, that he didn't want to study science. He'd said that he'd rather study history. Mehmet himself would rather have studied science, that is, if he had to study anything. He wouldn't have minded being an astronaut, but history — that was not for him.

The *dolmuş* bumped into the *dolmuş* park, and Mehmet and Korsan scrambled out. It would be easier to get to *Yenimahalle*, the district where Hayri was living, than he had expected. He asked a couple of people for directions and found out that he'd have to change buses only this once, and he eventually found the line where Yenimahalle was written on top of the old cars. The driver made him buy an extra ticket for Korsan, but agreed to tell him where to get off.

As the *dolmuş* pulled into Yenimahalle, Mehmet looked all around. It seemed very nice. There was a park with old people sitting on benches watching children riding tricycles along the paths between the grass. Probably Hayri and his parents came and sat here in the cool of the evening. *Çınar Sokak* was farther on, the park keeper said, watching zealously lest Mehmet put a foot on his grass. Mehmet walked on a bit, then spotted the street, just past a café. There was a fair-haired boy sitting at the café table eating an ice. Mehmet almost called out, but his mouth was too dry. Then the boy turned and he saw that it was only an ordinary boy like himself, and not Hayri at all.

Çınar Sokak was a little, leafy street with real *çınar* trees planted down its length. They were leaning over, shading the road. There were small houses with small gardens, some dry and bare but others with a profusion of green and flowers. There were children playing marbles and hopscotch in the road. A cat sat still and blinked slowly until she saw Korsan, and then she shot straight up one of the trees and peered down at them, trembling. Lucky Hayri — he always had been lucky.

Mehmet found Number 25, but he felt shy. A woman was sweeping the steps; she tipped clean water from a blue plastic jug and washed first one step and then another. Mehmet walked on past the house. He'd somehow thought that Hayri would be outside, and that they'd just meet up again. He wasn't prepared to have to knock and ask. The woman finished the steps, which gleamed in the sun. Her feet were pale and clean and wet with the water. She opened the low blue iron gate and swept the rest of the water out onto the street. Then she straightened up and looked right at Mehmet.

"And what do you want?" She stood solidly in the gateway on her flat white feet, and there were splashes of water up the front of her blue cotton dress.

"Nothing . . ."

"Well, then?" She started to close the gate with her cold eyes on Korsan.

"Is this . . . is this Hayri's house?"

"No, there's no Hayri here." She clicked the gate shut and turned to go in — a heavy, slow woman.

"Please, is this Number 25, Çınar Sokak?"

"Yes, but there's no Hayri here." She took the paper reluctantly and read the address. Then she said, as though she had only just thought of it, "But we bought the house in the spring, so I wouldn't know."

105

"Was there a fair boy living here then, a very fair boy?"

"Now you mention it, I think there was. A couple of old people and a boy had lived out the back. Odd sort of boy, would that be the one?"

"Different, maybe." Hayri had never struck him as odd.

The woman suddenly called very loudly to a neighbor, "Susan Hanım! Susan Hanım, here's somebody looking for that family that was here before us." She turned back to Mehmet and asked, "Friend of yours, was he?" Her eyes might have been less cold, but they were also mildly curious. "The family who used to live here," she called again to her neighbor, "didn't they have a boy, an odd boy?"

"Not them," the neighbor called back from the window above. "Those were their relatives, up from the country with that boy."

"Hayri?" asked Mehmet.

"Hayri, that's right, that was his name — shame really."

"What happened to him?"

"I don't know whether anything happened to him, but he wasn't right in the head, you could see it, like. Talked to himself, he did. Too much studying, it was. I never did hold with books. I always say it isn't natural, especially now there's the television. Gives people ideas, as though there aren't enough bad ideas in the world." It seemed as though she could talk for ever.

"But where did they go?" asked Mehmet.

"I don't know, though it can't have been far because I think I saw him the other day, down by the bazaar. Shame, wasn't it?"

"What was?" The slow woman was more interested now, scenting tragedy.

"You knew the old couple died, didn't you?"

"Here," said the woman in blue, to Mehmet. "You all right?" Mehmet nodded.

"Yes, you go and ask at the bazaar. They might know there."

Mehmet thanked them and retraced his steps, glancing neither into the park, nor to the café. It was midday, and the bazaar was crowded. It was hopeless. He trailed around, asking here and there. But everyone was busy selling tomatoes and peppers and weighing out kilos of dried beans; so who had time to remember a fair-haired boy called Hayri? He might as well go back. He would never find Hayri here. Perhaps he wasn't here to be found. Hadn't those women said "was" all the time? Something horrible must have happened, and he was not at all sure that he wanted to know about it. He called Korsan and began to push his way out. Twenty steps on, he sensed that Korsan had not followed him.

"Korsan, come here, boy, come!" Mehmet called. Korsan was standing still in the middle of the crowds.

"Korsan, here!" The dog looked at him but didn't move. Mehmet shouted this time, and people turned to stare. Korsan shook his big wrinkled head and started to edge backward. The crowd parted behind him. Mehmet felt in his pocket for the chain that he sometimes attached to Korsan's collar. Then the dog raised his head and barked. It was a deep, full bark. Women pulled their children out of the way, and bazaar men jumped behind their stalls.

"Here, you," said a woman. "If that's your dog, get him out of here."

"He doesn't look safe to me!" cried her friend. Now Korsan began to move forward. His nose was close to the ground. He moved on, then bounded between two stalls piled high with peaches.

"Look! There's a dog with rabies!" joked the peach seller, but he stepped aside so quickly that the peaches he was selling tipped out of his scales.

"Wretched rabid dog," he muttered, loudly enough for the men beside him to hear.

"Rabid dog! Look out!" yelled one excitedly. The cry passed from woman to woman. Korsan began to run. He loped along, barking. Mehmet ran after him, and the panic spread. People dropped their bags and ran. Korsan was making straight for the group of boys who carry away people's heavy bags in their wooden trucks. The boys shrieked and pushed each other, falling down among the carts. One boy, busy reading something, either didn't hear or didn't care, and Mehmet saw in horror that Korsan leaped straight onto the boy as though he would tear him to pieces. A horrified scream rose from the crowd as the boy fell to the ground, but no one moved to help him. Mehmet had nearly reached them when a voice from behind him cried, "Stand back! Stand back!" A policeman pushed through the crowd with his revolver in his hand, trying to take aim at Korsan.

"No!" screamed Mehmet. He pushed his way between the gun and the dog and cried "No!" again, shut his eyes very tight, and stood there. For a long time that must have been only a second, there was quiet, and then he heard

108

somebody say, "Korsan?" He opened his eyes, and there, getting up slowly, was Hayri. Korsan was leaping up at him again and again, his front paws resting easily on the boy's shoulders as he tried to lick his face and neck. If it *was* Hayri . . . They were Hayri's blue eyes, and it was like Hayri's voice, but changed — hoarse and jarring and as harsh as fingernails on the blackboard. Yet it was Hayri's voice that began an uncontrolled torrent of talking, explaining to the onlookers that it was his dog, that it was Korsan, that it was his Korsan, that Mehmet was looking after Korsan. . . . He talked on and on, with odd things thrown in as well, that he was studying and that some numbers were different from others and that . . . Then those who had gathered shook their heads and moved off grumbling to pick up their bags and finish their shopping. Mehmet, clipping the chain firmly onto Korsan, explained as best he could to the policeman.

"If I were you, lad, I'd get that dog and that crazy friend of yours out of this bazaar as quick as I could," said the policeman, who was only too pleased that the problem had resolved itself without his having to do anything. "I could have shot you, boy, and it wouldn't have been my fault. I'm not a good shot, you know."

Hayri was suddenly as quiet as he had been noisy. He rubbed his eyes as though they ached, and then he took a piece of paper from his pocket and began to read it. Mehmet took him by the arm, and the three of them walked off, with the iron wheels of the *tornet*s, or push-carts, screeching and groaning on the road behind them. Mehmet tried to think of something to say.

"You know that place that you told me about, the

109

plains where all the horses galloped over the grass? Well, I'm living near there." Hayri didn't look up from his paper. He walked on in silence. He didn't answer any of Mehmet's questions. He didn't seem to hear. He didn't put out a hand to Korsan. He moved one broken shoe in front of the other. It was as though he weren't there.

But he was there — Mehmet could smell him. At first Mehmet thought he must have stepped in some dog's dirt. He looked under his shoe, and then he realized that it was Hayri. Hayri smelled awful. He wasn't very clean himself, he knew; his fingernails were black and his head itched, but it wasn't like Hayri. Hayri was covered in dirt. The skin of his hands was black. The ugly blisters around his eyes and mouth ran into dark bruises on his face. Something yellow and sticky had run down out of his ears and stuck itself in his hair. It was a Hayri that Mehmet had never, ever dreamed of. There were some very poor children in the shantytown, but he had never seen anything like this. He felt sick and shocked; he wanted to get away. He wished he hadn't come. He would have passed Hayri by and never recognized him if it hadn't been for Korsan. Freckles had been right: he shouldn't have brought the dog. He let go of Hayri's arm. Freckles was right — everybody was right, except him. Even his mother could be right, and about the jacket, too. At least Hakan didn't stink. He had to get away.

"Look, Hayri, I expect you've got to get back to the bazaar, and you've got your studying to do . . . those numbers to look at. . . . It was nice to see you again. . . ." He looked very closely at Hayri's ugly, hurt face. The blue eyes were fastened on Mehmet's lips and never raised

110

themselves to look him in the eye. That made it easier. If Hayri had forgotten him, he'd go. He did. He walked away from his friend, away down the road, and he didn't look back. Just before the *dolmuş* stand, Korsan dragged back against the chain. Suddenly he was fighting the collar and chain with all his strength. He twisted his head swiftly and then he was free — running, leaping, bounding back to Hayri.

"Ungrateful dog," said Mehmet bitterly. Well, if he felt like that, he was welcome to go.

He had done his best. Why, Hayri had not even said his name. If Hayri and Korsan loved each other so much, they could look after each other, too. He'd had enough.

When he got back to Şentepe, he bought himself an ice cream with the money he had saved on Korsan's return fare. He sat on a box outside the grocer and licked slowly and hoped that Hakan would come past and see him. But nobody gave him a second glance. The ice cream tasted too sweet, and it melted too quickly and ran down his hand, and when he went to lick it off, he was disgusted by the foul smell that now clung to him. He felt sick with himself and with Hayri and with everything. He made for home and hoped, secretly, that his parents would not notice anything and would be pleased to see him.

·{ 8 }·

IT'S VERY HARD to understand people sometimes. There wasn't one member of Mehmet's family who hadn't grumbled about Korsan at some time: he ate too much, he frightened people, he chased the neighbor's chickens, he made muddy footprints, he brought in fleas. . . . Yet now, when Mehmet came home alone without Korsan, he was met by disbelieving and disapproving disgust. He couldn't even explain to them how it had happened, because he didn't want to tell them about Hayri. He twisted the empty collar round and round in his hands and waited for someone to say that it was probably for the best or that it was bound to happen someday or that Korsan was, after all, only a dog. But they didn't. Even Osman looked up sourly from moving the rest of his and Elif's things to their new house and remarked that Mehmet was a careless fool.

"If you were going to do such a stupid thing as lose the

112

dog, you could at least have given him to me, and I'd have sold him. I could have got twenty thousand for him. A man at the bank was interested."

Then Mehmet's father joined in: "Really, Mehmet, first you lose my tools, valuable tools that I've had all my life and that I'm sure to need again soon, and now you lose that dog that was worth a lot of money. Tomorrow it will be something else, without a doubt. I don't know why we bother with you. You're out on the streets all day, and what is your mother doing all this time? Altering Hakan's jacket for you and ruining her eyes. And you don't even notice. Yusuf Amca is right: 'The cane comes from Heaven.'"

"Poor Korsan!" cried Mehmet's little sister, Hatice. "He'll be lost, and a truck will run him over and kill him!" Then several of them began to sniff loudly.

Mehmet could not think what to say. If he had found the words, they would not have listened. They wouldn't have understood. People didn't hear. Then he thought of Hayri, who did not seem to hear either. He looked fiercely at the hated dark blue jacket. It lay on his mother's lap; if he concentrated hard enough on hating it, it would keep him from crying. He could see a ridge all down the back where she had taken a tuck. She held it out to him, smiling, forcing him with her smile to try it on. It was still too big. It was a hateful, cut-down jacket, and he felt caught in it the way a mouse feels caught in a trap. But at this moment, when he knew that they were all against him, he knew that he could not say that he hated the jacket.

113

"My son," said his mother, inspecting her small stitches with pride, "you will look as smart as the next boy. Now, listen to your mother. Tomorrow, take this collar back to the lady who gave it to you — I've always said you should not accept things from strangers. Take it back. Then go and get your father's tools for him and go round and thank your aunt for this jacket, and everything will be all right, you'll see."

"I promise — everything will be all right," added his father.

Mehmet nodded because there was nothing for him to say.

Mehmet's head ached. It ached so much that he could not leave his mattress. Every noise made it worse. They moved him into the little empty room opposite them and came and stood around him, but they couldn't think of anything to do. When his head ached less, he slept, and when it ached more, he pretended to sleep. Sometimes he heard the shouts of the soccer players, but he didn't want to go and play. Freckles came and said that he was sorry about Korsan, but Mehmet rolled over to face the wall and wouldn't talk. Once he thought he heard an argument, his father and Ayşe shouting, with his father's voice getting angrier and Ayşe's voice remaining hard, cool, and determined. Then he slept again. Each time when he slept, his peace was broken by the barking and howling of wild dogs. The puppies of the spring now roamed hungry and dangerous through the shantytown. He dreamed of them: they became great red-eyed beasts that leaped at

114

you and got you down and held you there in the dust
with no one to hear your cries.

Then he woke up one morning, clear-headed. There
was no pain. He had to go and find Hayri; that was as
clear to him now as the day was bright. It was early. He
could leave before anyone awoke. Only when he had
done that could he sort out the other things. He would
find the tools, give back the collar — he'd even wear the
jacket — but they were not important at the moment. It
was going back and finding his friend that was important.

Outside it was cool and quiet. The rising sun made the
clouds of dust and smoke over the city glow pink. He was
surprised and pleased to see Ayşe hurrying down the path
in front of him.

"Ayşe, wait for me," he called, hurrying with an awkward early morning stiffness. She was startled by his
voice, but pleased to see him up and well again. She
looked very pretty — not as pretty as Elif, but, then, sisters were different, and anyway, she was nice to look at.
She was altered, too, but perhaps it was just the light of
the new day that made her look taller and straighter.

"Ayşe Abla," he panted, grabbing her hand. She would
listen to him — he was sure of it. She put her arm around
him and cuddled him to her as though he were a very
little boy.

"About Korsan," he breathed into her shoulder, and
then having begun, he had to tell her all about it. He could
no longer pretend that nothing had happened.

"We'll find him," she said.

"It isn't just Korsan," he whispered.

"What is it, then?"

"It's Hayri." And he began to explain.

He saw tears in her dark eyes, but she only said again, "Then we'll find them, both of them." She brushed away her tears, and then her scarf with its little edge of flowers fell back and he saw why she looked altered: she had cut off the two long braids that had hung down below her waist.

"Why did you do that?" Even his grandmother still had her long hair, though it was as gray and thin as newly spun wool.

"I sold it. A woman at work told me how."

"Why?"

"There were things they needed."

"Who?"

"Them," she said and nodded toward the crooked door of Muhlis's house.

"You shouldn't go there alone, Ayşe Abla. You mustn't go there alone, not now that Ramazan is there." They both knew what he meant, but she did not alter her step. "You can't — I'll tell father."

"You won't." She smiled down at him steadily, and they both knew that of course he wouldn't tell his father or anyone else. Then he brightened up.

"But you're not alone, are you? I'm with you!"

Suddenly they were laughing as though they were children back in the village, creeping out to lick the creamy top from the milk before they were seen. She pinched his cheek and whispered hotly into his ear that he could come with her if he promised not to tell Fatma Teyze! They were both giggling into their hands when she knocked softly on the crazy door. Then he saw what she had done.

Muhlis was still asleep, but instead of the muddle of dirty, tumbled rubbish on which he had been lying when Mehmet last saw him, there was now a new green quilt edged with a new white sheet. And Muhlis's long head lay on a new white pillow. There was a band of embroidered flowers on the pillow, and they looked so bright and fresh that Mehmet felt he wanted to pick them. The bags and boxes had been cleared from the corner, and in their place stood a small blue table and four blue chairs. Ayşe took from her bag a small pile of new bowls and dishes and set them down as quietly as she could on the table. It all looked so nice that you almost forgot the floor was made of stamped earth and that Ramazan was curled in a rug in a corner like a dog. Mehmet almost stumbled over him and felt shy of this tall, quiet man who pushed aside the blanket and rose to his feet without saying a word.

Ayşe did not seem shy; she talked to him like an old friend. She told him not to forget Muhlis's medicine and not to let him get tired, and then she was gone again, down the dusty track, and Ramazan came outside and watched her until she was gone from view. Still he said nothing. He filled the kettle and began to set out bread and olives for their breakfast. Mehmet moved awkwardly from place to place. He seemed to be in the way here. That was strange, when Ayşe seemed so at home.

"Mehmet!" Muhlis had woken and was sitting propped up against the flowery pillow. "Ayşe said that my foot is much better and that I can get up tomorrow. We're going to have a picnic. Ramazan is going to take us out in the cart, aren't you, Ramazan? We're going out to that place where all the herds of horses were, you know, before it all got dry and dusty. We're going to have a picnic there. Yıldız and Korsan can have a real day's holiday. It was going to be a surprise, but I had to tell you. It'll be on a Sunday, won't it, Ramazan, when Ayşe Abla doesn't have to work? Ramazan says there's a stream there, with real, clean water — that's right, isn't it, Ramazan?"

Ramazan agreed, and Mehmet stared at Muhlis in horror. So, he didn't know about Korsan. All this time, Ayşe must have been expecting him to go out and find the dog. He hurried out into the sharp light, and Ramazan followed him.

"You'd better find that dog of yours. Nothing should be out on these streets alone, not even a dog." He was right of course, just as Ayşe had been right. Mehmet started to run down the track to the main road.

He searched for two days without success. He crossed the city again to Yenimahalle and went from café to café and from shop to shop. He asked every beggar and stopped every gang of youths. He sought out the same policeman and the man who had been selling peaches in the bazaar. They all said the same: they had not seen *deli* Hayri around for a day or two.

"Don't worry," said one. "You know what they say: 'A bitter eggplant is not hurt by the frost.'"

Then one of the child porters at the bazaar said that he thought he knew where *deli* Hayri slept at night. He was a little dwarflike boy with old gray eyes in a creased face.

"What'll you give me if I show you?" he asked in a shrill, squeaky voice.

"I'll give you five hundred," said Mehmet.

"It isn't worth it. I'll miss my place in the line."

"A thousand?"

"Let's see it."

"Here," Mehmet showed the corner of a bill, and the dwarf passed his tongue over his lips and then set off, dodging between the stalls. The dwarf scampered through the crowd with the skill of a rat. Once or twice Mehmet thought he saw him snatch a fruit and hide it in his clothes, but he moved so quickly that Mehmet was never sure. Mehmet was breathless trying to keep up. He kept slipping on the garbage on the ground and banging into indignant women. Then the dwarf climbed through what seemed to have been a hole in the wall of an old open-air cinema.

"There were several of us that lived here last winter," the dwarf called over his shoulder. "Your friend lived here. See?" He pointed up at what had been the screen and where, on the fine summer evenings of other summers, there had been pictures of heroes and heroines. "That's where he did his lessons, well, that's what he called them. Mad he was, not a bad chap, but mad all the same."

The screen was covered with writing and numbers. There were poems and mathematics and the dates of the War of Independence and maps of the continents and

119

the names of the sultans — all poured out, one on top of the other.

"I think he used his brain up writing all that. All that studying isn't good for you," said the dwarf. "You want to see where he slept?" Mehmet was not sure that he did, but he said yes, and the dwarf went through a small opening under the screen.

"Caw!" he said, backing out quickly with his hand over his nose. "You can have a look, but don't ask me to." Mehmet crouched down and crawled in. His hands touched things in the dark. It smelled so bad he could hardly breathe. He lit a match and saw in its briefly flickering light that he was in an animal's lair: it was a little concrete cave, and it was filled with paper. There were newspapers, magazines, books, advertisements, and thousands and thousands of paper scraps. They must have been picked up from the streets and bazaars and smoothed out and piled up one on top of the other from the floor to the ceiling. There must have been thousands of them, and in one place you could see the flattened-out hollow where someone had curled up and slept. Mehmet crawled out.

"That was your friend's place, then, was it?"

"I think so," he said, though he was sure, for sticking on his own hand were pale dog's hairs.

"Then, if you don't mind, I'll have my thousand and be getting back to work." Mehmet handed the bill to him.

"You don't happen to have a cigarette as well?"

"No."

"Shame. Shame about your friend. He wasn't so bad until the fire."

"What fire?"

"The fire with all them papers. Some of the boys thought they'd play a joke on him. Light a corner, you know. We didn't think he'd mind that much, but he did. He was very upset, said he used those papers for studying and that we had burned up his chances."

"Did he get burned, too?"

"Not much. You couldn't get a good blaze up in there. Nothing much would live in there, not even a fire." The dwarf laughed.

"Do you think he'll come back?"

"How should I know?" said the dwarf, picking up a cigarette butt from the ground.

Mehmet waited until it was dark, but no one came back to the empty cinema. Then he wandered away through the deserted bazaar, where women were searching in the piles of garbage for things to eat. He supposed that Hayri must have come here in the evenings, scavenging not for something to eat but for something to read.

That night Mehmet's bad dreams returned. He dreamed of a huge dog barking and barking, and he was trying to get away, burrowing deeper and deeper into some papers. The dog was coming after him, and he was trying to put the papers between himself and the dog, but they kept tearing in his hands and he could never get enough of them. The dog was barking more loudly, and he reached for some more papers — and rolled off his mattress onto the concrete floor.

There really were dogs barking outside. It was a dreadful dog fight. He looked out of the window. Neighbors shouted. He heard windows pulled up and the thud of stones flung at the animals. Then he heard running footsteps and the swish and smack of water thrown from a bucket. The fight seemed to be breaking up. He craned far out but could see nothing, only hear the yelps and the sound of claws breaking on stone. Then one dog was howling in pain, and its cry became fainter as it made its desperate escape from its tormentors. The pack moved on to awaken other sleepers, and finally Mehmet slept, too.

But suddenly he was awake again. He did not know if it was hours later or only minutes. Something else had woken him. Mehmet was trying so hard to hear that he barely breathed. Then he dozed. Then he heard it: a sound from the darkness like a long sigh. There it was again . . . then nothing . . . then there it was, three times. There was something down there in the dust waiting for him. Little Hatice and Ali must have heard it, too, for their muttered, sleepy voices came to him, and then he heard his mother sleepily soothing them back to sleep. It gave him the courage to get up.

In the first light that was giving shape and color back to the world, Mehmet saw Korsan lying at the base of the wall and hurried over to him. He felt his dry, cracked nose. Then his hand touched torn skin, and he realized that Korsan had been savaged by the pack of dogs. Why had he not defended himself? Perhaps there had been too many, even for a dog as strong as Korsan. He must have been exhausted, too, for he must have been searching for the way home for days. How had he done it? It should be impossible, yet you read of things like this in the papers. He and Hayri had once read a story in a children's book about a dog and a cat who had traveled thousands of miles to find their old home. And Hayri? Where was he, then? Mehmet put his arms around Korsan and whispered to him, "Hayri, where is he?"

Korsan dragged himself to his feet and, with his head hardly above the ground, started forward. Then Mehmet saw Hayri and shuddered. He was crouched behind two overturned garbage bins. Mehmet guessed that the dogs had come deep into the shantytown at night, searching for scraps and had come upon Hayri and Korsan. Korsan, in order to draw the dogs away from the boy, must have let himself be attacked.

Hayri crept from his hiding place and drew a pile of neatly folded papers from his jacket pocket.

"I just thought I'd get on with my lessons," he said in that strange, harsh voice. He smoothed out the page and began to read it. Mehmet, looking over his shoulder, saw that it was part of a page about the Mongol horsemen of old. Hayri stood there by the garbage bins and studied history, and for a moment Mehmet was paralyzed with horror.

Morning was approaching, and he knew that he must get help, for without it, Hayri would not survive. The rising sun was casting its shadows, and the flies, soaking up the first warmth, began to twitch their wings and fly down on to the rubbish. He had to get help and soon, before the shantytown awoke. He could hear voices and the splash of water in a basin. A boy in somebody else's red plastic slippers stumbled awkwardly down the track. He stopped and rubbed the sleep from his unwashed face.

He stuck a finger in his nose and fished around for last night's dried crusts, and then he saw Mehmet, Hayri, and Korsan. The little boy came close, scratching and picking carefully, then squatted down and looked at Hayri with interest. Then he flicked something off his finger at him and ran away chuckling, with the great red slippers thumping up clouds of dust. Mehmet had to take them away, but where? And who, in all the world, would help?

Then he thought of Zekiye Hanım. If anyone could help him, she — in her white house where the water always flowed — she could help him. He put out a hand and began to lead Hayri slowly away. On the day of the storm, hadn't she stood alone in that dreadful wind and watched them go, when everyone else had hidden behind their shuttered windows? She must help them. Hadn't she almost said that she would? He tightened his grip on Hayri's arm, making him walk faster. They had to get away. Yes, those had been her words: "If I can do anything, if I can ever do anything, I promise, by the name of God, that I will." She had said it. They passed the door behind which Muhlis and Ramazan must be sleeping. That was where he could leave Korsan. He pointed to the door.

"Stay, Korsan, stay." Korsan looked up at him with reproachful, distrustful eyes, but he lay down by the door with his head resting on his front paws. Ramazan would know what to do about the wound. Looking back at Korsan, Hayri hesitated, but Mehmet urged him on.

"Look," he said. "I know an old lady who has a lot of books that you can read." He was not sure if Hayri heard, but he began to walk more quickly. It was true, well, almost true. That day when he and Zekiye Hanım had talked about books and the garden, she had said that she would like to meet Hayri.

He untied Yıldız, heaved Hayri up onto her back, and scrambled up behind and clicked his tongue. She worried and fussed a bit and then settled down to their weight and began a stiff, unaccustomed canter. On the main road, Yıldız slowed down of her own accord to a trot and then to a walk. There was scarcely anyone on the streets, only a few children coming back from the bakery, clutching loaves of hot bread, a man searching through the garbage bins with a long pole, and a handful of laborers waiting for the first bus to take them into the city. They turned and stared after the two boys on the horse. Mehmet, seeing their reflection in the dusty window of a roadside garage, stared, too. They looked like a couple of scarecrows. He wasn't as filthy as Hayri, but his old clothes had been washed so often that they hardly had any color left in them. He was tattered and patched, and his toes stuck out of his split shoes. His hair was longer than it had ever been before. What if the old lady should close her door in their face? Where would he go then? What if she saw them from behind her heavy lace curtains, and never even answered their knock! She might stay there, in her peaceful, elegant room and read her books and breathe in the perfume of the late roses until she heard them go away.

Hayri was stiff and awkward on the horse. If he had not been so light, he would have fallen several times. Mehmet gripped him firmly and felt that he was as thin and bony as a young stork. He made an odd crackling and rustling noise, and when Mehmet had to catch him suddenly round the waist to stop him sliding off Yıldız's back, he realized that Hayri's clothes were all packed with more pieces of paper.

The sun had risen, and their shadows moved short and sharp on the softening tarmac. It was getting hotter and hotter. The sweat ran down the back of Hayri's dirty neck, leaving a greasy trail, and a noisy fly buzzed over them.

They were almost outside the house. Yıldız's iron shoes rang too loudly along the street. Somebody might turn them away; this was a good district after all. A man was washing a big silver car in front of a house; he was washing and washing, and when he turned to watch them go past, the clear water poured out of the hose and ran on down the street, where it washed the gutters very clean.

At last they were there. Even before Mehmet pushed open the gate, he could hear the fall of a fine, free spray of water on the softening earth. The garden bloomed and shone in its late summer glory. It smelled of fallen apples and ripening grapes. Now that his hand was on the gate, he was struck by fear and doubt. Suppose Ramazan was wrong and you could not read people the way you could read books? Perhaps he had been mistaken about Zekiye Hanım. Perhaps she was really like his uncle and aunt, whose fine words were no more real than their ugly red carpet. She may not have really meant it when she had said she would help any time. But it was too late to turn back. He could see Zekiye Hanım at the end of the garden, walking between her roses and choosing which to cut and take indoors. She cut a stem, then saw him and smiled. Mehmet went down the garden and bent over her hand, kissed it and touched it to his forehead, then stepped aside so that she might see Hayri, who had trailed in and sat down on the bottom step. He was rocking to and fro with his knees pressed up against his chest.

"But that's not Muhlis, surely," she said, with the cut rose held very tightly in her pale, wrinkled hand.

"No, that's my other friend, the one I told you about, the one called Hayri, the clever one who came here to study." Had she remembered? "He's . . . he's the one who read all those books." He nearly reminded her that she had promised, on the day of the storm, to help if he ever needed her, but he didn't say it. With Hayri sitting there on the steps, tracing the gold veins in the polished stone, there did not seem to Mehmet much more that he could say.

"But what has happened to him?" She spoke so softly that he did not know if he was even meant to answer. Zekiye Hanım went slowly, slowly forward, and then suddenly she was almost running. She went straight past Hayri and out of the gate into the road.

"Dr. Bey," she called down the street. "Dr. Bey, come quickly!" He had never heard her shout. She had never even spoken loudly before. Mehmet was scared to hear her old voice calling down the street. She was going to turn them out. He should not have come. He was a fool. Why should she help?

"It's all right, Zekiye Hanım," he said. "We shouldn't have come. We'll go." He started to pull savagely at Hayri's jacket. He wanted to get him away. He wanted to get him out of the garden before that man came in from the street and drove them off like dogs.

127

"Dr. Bey, hurry," she called again, and the man who had been washing the car strode in through the gate.

"Dr. Bey, you must help me. I have a sick boy here, and I need you to tell me what to do." She was very distressed.

"It doesn't matter," said Mehmet, still pulling at Hayri. Why, a man like that might get the police to them. "We'll go. We shouldn't be here."

"Oh, but you should," said Zekiye Hanım, laying her hand on his shoulder. "You should be here. I let you go away once, on the day of the storm, and I've regretted it ever since. I should have helped you more then, but I didn't. Now this time I can and I shall."

"But this isn't Muhlis," said Mehmet. He could not have borne a misunderstanding.

"No, I know this isn't Muhlis," she said, "but I don't think that makes much difference, does it?"

"I don't know," he mumbled, looking down at the ground. It shouldn't matter, not to him, but it often seemed important to other people. The doctor clearly had his doubts.

"Do you really want me to take him into the house?" he asked, shaking his head. "Why don't I take him into one of the hospitals for you? I'll take him myself."

"Thank you, but I want you to take him into the house for me," she said. The doctor shook his head some more and swore to himself in a quiet sort of way, but his hand was gentle and firm as he helped Hayri up the marble steps.

Mehmet sat and waited in the kitchen. Zekiye Hanım had put out milk, bread, and white cheese for him, but he didn't touch them. He could hear them moving about upstairs. Water ran and ran in the bathroom; their footsteps moved from one room to another, and drawers were pulled out and shut. Mehmet broke off tiny bits of bread and rolled them into pellets, but he couldn't eat them. What were they doing to Hayri? He looked around the kitchen with all its shining glass and china and its floor so clean you could have eaten off it. No sounds came from above. He went to the foot of the stairs, which were carpeted in gray wool. Now he could hear their voices, very low and quick, but not Hayri's. He started impatiently up the stairs, but they came out of one of the bedrooms, and the old lady put her finger to her lips and hurried down to him.

"I think I'd better take him home now — you know, because my other friend will be worried about his horse . . ."

"You can't take him home, Mehmet."

"Why not? What have you done to him?"

"He's a very, very sick boy," said the man, and putting his arm around Mehmet, took him out on to the balcony. "If you hadn't brought him here, I don't know how long he would have survived, not out there."

"Ahmet Bey is a doctor. You could not have done better than bring your friend here."

"Is he really that ill? I mean, I know he needed a wash, but he was still studying . . . I don't know what happened. . . ."

"None of us knows how it happens, that a boy like that who is clearly so special, is thrown out on the streets, like yesterday's garbage," said Zekiye Hanım sadly.

129

"I know! I know quite well," began Ahmet Bey, excitedly. "The city is crawling with children like this!" Mehmet looked at him in surprise: he had never heard a grown-up talk like this. Ramazan, yes, he talked like this, but not an educated person. You did not expect people like this to get excited over anything much.

"Now, dear Ahmet Bey, we can't go into that now," said Zekiye Hanım, in that very firm and decided way that elderly folk sometimes have. She turned to Mehmet. "We need to know all that you know about your friend." They asked him about Hayri's family. Had any of them acted strangely? Had Hayri been different from the other boys in the village? Did he have brothers and sisters who were different?

Mehmet began to explain how Hayri was different, how he had always been different; how the schoolteacher had told Hayri's parents that he must go away because he was too clever. Ahmet Bey listened and took off his glasses and fiddled with them, then put them on again and asked more questions, and Mehmet found himself telling more to these two strangers than he had ever told anyone before. The doctor leaned forward with his elbows on his knees and passed his glasses from hand to hand and shook his head. When Mehmet described the old cinema where Hayri had been sleeping, Ahmet Bey stood up restlessly and paced the balcony and shook his head more and more.

"I could have told them how it would be, right back in the village," Mehmet said.

"What do you mean?" asked Zekiye Hanım.

"I mean," said Mehmet, "I mean . . ." But when it

came to it, he could not find the words, not here, in this house, where the water flowed day and night, and not to Zekiye Hanım, with her fine, troubled face. She had been kinder and better than anyone he had ever known, but you cannot tell these people everything.

Ahmet Bey explained to Mehmet that one of the reasons that Hayri had been behaving so strangely was because he had gone deaf. Colds, illness, dirt, and maybe blows to the head had damaged his ears so much that at the moment he couldn't hear. Ahmet Bey was sure that in a week or two, with the right medicines, this would be cured. He was not yet sure what else was wrong with Hayri. That was why he wanted to keep him here to look after him.

"But you can't do that," said Mehmet.

"Why not?"

"He's not, well, he's not your family. . . ." It sounded rather stupid, but they didn't laugh at him.

"He's not my family. That's true. But I think I can still do something for him, and you must let me do that this time," said Zekiye Hanım. "It doesn't seem a great deal to ask of you: to let me give shelter to someone who needs it. Won't you let me do that much?" He did not quite understand what she meant.

"Look," said Ahmet Bey, "perhaps you know the story of the two trees that were blown by the storm. One bent lower and lower, and though all its leaves were blown away and its branches were broken, it survived the storm. The other tree refused to bend: it stood up as straight as it could and pretended that there wasn't a storm. In the end it suddenly broke. It split in two, was uprooted, and

died. Your friend is like the second tree, and you found
him and brought him here to us just before he was split
in two. But he needs to be protected from the storms;
perhaps he'll always need to be. And that is what Zekiye
Hanım wants to do for him. You must let her."

Mehmet could see that he really had no choice. He followed Zekiye Hanım upstairs to look at Hayri. He was
already asleep, and yes, that was Hayri again. Though he
was so thin and ill, it was Hayri all right. Hayri with his
fair, bright hair and delicate face that was so different from
Mehmet's own, which was round and dark and not special at all. If you hadn't known, you might have thought
that Hayri belonged here with these quiet, serious people.
Mehmet turned away; he had to get back.

"Would you like me to drive you home?" asked Ahmet
Bey. Yes, of course he would have liked it, and he would
have made sure that they drove past Hakan's house and
that everybody saw him in that huge, silver car, but no,
such things weren't for him, it seemed. He had to ride
Yıldız back through the scorched streets.

"Thanks, but I'd rather ride," he said, then went out to
where Yıldız was waiting patiently.

·{ 9 }··

MEHMET expected his family to be anxiously waiting for him. He was prepared for them to be angry and upset. Somebody must have seen him early that morning. That child in the slippers had surely told his mother. He knew that news spreads through the shanty-town like fire in a haystack. And maybe that wouldn't have been such a bad thing: they had to know that he had found Hayri, and now, for the first time, he was sure that he had done something right. Zekiye Hanım and Ahmet Bey had said that he'd done the right thing, so though his family might grumble, they must agree in the end. He had been right to go back and find his friend. Let them shout a bit — he didn't mind. He slipped from Yıldız's back and went up the stairs two at a time.

They looked up at him and then away as though he were of no more importance than a shadow cast into the room by a passing cloud. No one asked him where he had been, though he had been gone all day. Surely they weren't still angry about the tools?

"Korsan came back last night," he said. His grandfather turned slowly from the window and nodded and then turned back and stared far into the distance as though he would see beyond the mountains.

"I expect you heard the fight. He was really hurt by that pack of dogs," Mehmet tried again. His mother might at least be interested.

"Mehmet," she said, not looking at him. "Mehmet, you can't go back to school. We can't afford to send you." Now what had happened? He searched each face but found no answer. His mother couldn't be still fussing about the clothes, could she?

"If it's the jacket . . ." he tried.

"It's not the jacket, or the books. . . ." She tried to explain but couldn't, and then they all joined in, interrupting each other and crying, his mother and father, his grandmother and his grandfather — even Ali and Hatice joined in. Only Ayşe sat on her own, watching them with contempt and stitching away fiercely.

Fatma Teyze had visited them for tea that afternoon, his mother said, but it seemed that she had something else on her mind. She had told them that Yusuf Bey was worried about them. Now it was summer, but soon it would be winter, and winter in Ankara was cold, very cold. Yusuf Bey was a kind man, Fatma Teyze had reminded them, a religious man, who took his responsibilities as a landlord very seriously. He would never allow anybody to say that he had let his relatives spend a winter in Ankara in a house without windows. Yusuf had been very offended, she said, that Osman and Elif had moved out as if the house was not fit to be lived in. No, he would not let anyone suffer, so, they were going to put windows in the house! Now, Fatma Teyze went on, everybody knows that Yusuf has a heart of gold, so he had decided that while he was putting in windows, he would also connect the water and electricity.

At first they had been overjoyed. Mehmet's mother had never lived in a house with running water. Now she could keep them all clean and wash clothes whenever she liked. She could wash clothes several times a day if she wanted to. Mehmet's father had reminded her that although she had never trusted him, he had known that everything would turn out all right. He'd get that washing machine that he'd promised her. Look, he'd said, he had been right, or almost so; they could have left the red plastic basin back in the village! Aunt Fatma had smiled and sipped her tea and said why not? Everybody hoped to have a washing machine these days.

They had made fresh tea, and Hatice had gone dancing and singing to the grocers to buy chocolate cookies to celebrate the good news. Fatma Teyze, who had a weakness for chocolate, had dipped the cookies in her tea and told them that Yusuf Amca felt they deserved a written lease to give them the same protection as his other tenants. They had protested, saying that they trusted Yusuf Bey — his word was good enough for them. No, Fatma Teyze had been firm; Yusuf didn't want it to be said that he treated his relatives less well than other people. They could have a contract like all the other people who lived in their houses. Naturally, once there were windows and water

135

and lights, then the block could be rented to other people, too.

And then she had brought out a rent agreement for them to sign. This way they would all know where they stood, she had said. Mehmet's father, who could just sign his name but certainly could not read, had called for a pen and had scratched his name with pride. Fatma Teyze had congratulated them on being proper tenants at last and had told them that the workmen would start in the morning. Yusuf Amca would be coming home for his supper shortly and expected it to be served the moment he arrived, so, if they did not mind, she must be getting on home.

It was only when Ayşe came home and read the paper carefully that they realized they had agreed to pay more in rent than Mehmet's father earned in a month. Then they had cried and wailed and bemoaned their bad luck. But they never thought of going straight round and tearing up the paper and throwing the pieces down. That was what Mehmet would have done: he would have thrown them down, all over Fatma Teyze's red carpet.

Mehmet's father refused to see that he had made a mistake. They had dried their tears and set about planning. They decided that if Mehmet and his mother both started work, then they could just about manage. If Mehmet just worked this year, he could go back to school next year. It was not what they had dreamed of, but they did not seem to have much choice.

Mehmet was relieved to find out that that was all it was. He didn't mind about the school. It was his family who was so eager for him to go anyway. He almost smiled: now he wouldn't have to wear the jacket! He knew what he would do; he'd sell the jacket with Muhlis. No, he didn't mind about school one little bit, and from what he had seen and heard about Hayri, studying did not seem to be such a good idea. He didn't really believe that you could use your brains up, but it didn't seem worth the risk.

"That's all right. I'm happy to work," he said to his parents. They looked pleased again and grateful, and then they told him the good news. Yusuf Amca had sent Hakan round with a message just a few minutes earlier to say that Mehmet and his mother could start work at the workshop on Monday morning.

"I said I'd work, but I didn't say I'd work for him," said Mehmet. They might be fools, but he wasn't.

"Mehmet, my son, it's a wonderful opportunity. You'll learn the trade the proper way. You'll be a skilled tailor," protested his eager father.

"How's that? I thought I could go back to school next year."

"Don't talk to me like that, or I'll whip you." His father turned on him sullenly.

"I won't go."

"You'll do what I say!"

"I tell you, I won't go."

"You'll go if I have to beat you unconscious and drag you there myself!" His father leaped to his feet and struck Mehmet a blow on his cheek that knocked him to the floor.

"I won't, I won't! You can kill me but I won't!"

"You can and you will!" His father raised his arm again.

It was not his mother who stepped in between them but Ayşe. When Mehmet thought about it afterward, he realized that in that single moment one of those ties that binds you so tightly to your mother had been broken. He got to his feet and faced his father.

"How much did Yusuf Amca say he would pay?"

"Fifteen thousand, my son, and maybe he'll make it more. I'll ask him tomorrow — I promise." His father was already ashamed of his bad temper. He was eager to make peace and to forget everything. But Mehmet didn't want to forget. His mother brought a damp cloth to put on his swelling cheek, but he stepped out of her reach.

"I'll bring you your fifteen thousand, father. I'll even try and bring you seventeen thousand, but I'm not going to work for Yusuf Amca. Never." Then he went into the opposite room and took out Korsan's collar and went down to where Yıldız was still waiting.

If this was victory, he didn't think much of it, and he had not enjoyed the battle. And then he remembered that they still had not bothered to ask him where he had been all day. Several children were hanging around talking to Yıldız and stroking her. They knew that she had been missing all day, for nothing much goes unremarked in the shantytown. Now they were happy to see her back. They stroked her nose with their darting little brown hands. One small girl had brought her half an apple and was coaxing her to eat it so she could grow fat and strong. As Mehmet led Yıldız down the track to Muhlis's house, the children followed, flanking him in an admiring group. They argued mildly with each other about who could say the nicest things about Yıldız, and they pushed each other a bit to see who could dare to walk the closest to her hooves. When they got to Muhlis's door, one of them pretended to blow a trumpet to deliver the good news of Yıldız's safe return.

This time Mehmet felt like a hero, and the feeling was nicer because he had not beaten anyone to enjoy this victory. There was Muhlis, limping out to rub his face against Yıldız's. The horse made small blowing noises, swished her tail, and stamped her feet, making the children scatter laughingly into the shadows. Ramazan was there, too, and grumbled fiercely that he had been out everywhere looking for Mehmet, and there was Korsan, with a neat white bandage around his middle, wagging his stumpy tail from side to side.

It felt very good to sit outside on a box and drink hot sweet tea and to be listened to. Once Mehmet thought he saw Hakan watching them from the shadows, but he wasn't sure, and he reminded himself that now he didn't care either. He wasn't like Hayri, and he wasn't going to be uprooted — not by anyone.

Muhlis still wanted to go on the picnic. It didn't make any difference that Mehmet had quarreled with his family.

"It just shows you," Muhlis said, "that I was right. I sometimes wondered whether I had extra bad luck with my family, but look at yours now. Not all of them — I mean — Ayşe Abla is different." He glanced quickly at his brother. Mehmet didn't know what to say. Ramazan continued to sort out his cans and bottles in a noisy sort of way that told you that he could have said a great deal if he cared to.

"Still, like I said, the picnic is a holiday for Yıldız and Korsan, so we can't say we're not going. It's not *our* picnic!"

They planned it for the next Sunday. It was to be a secret, but of course, word got around. Freckles was quite clear about it: he didn't ask them if he could come but told them that he was coming, and bringing his younger brother, too. His mother had promised that if he took his little brother out from under her feet for a whole Sunday, she would make them some special food to take on the picnic. And Mehmet didn't see why he shouldn't take Hatice and Ali since it had been a miserable summer for them. Elif, hearing that Ayşe was to go on a trip without her, was angry, but prettily so, and sent a message that she was astonished that they even thought of going without her. Then the children who hung around Muhlis's place made it clear that they wanted to come. They didn't dare to ask straight out, but they made it clear by hanging around even more. Muhlis, limping down to see Yıldız, was accompanied by a crowd of small helpers. Nobody wanted to miss anything. It was like a siege, but they enjoyed it. Sometimes they teased the children and said that they had already been and come back, and that the picnic was over, but the children were too clever, or not clever enough.

"That's not true! We watched you all day yesterday!"

"Did you, indeed?"

"No, we didn't. Yes, we did, but you didn't see us, did you?"

"No, never." They laughed.

They saw Hakan, too. He was always around. He and

Mehmet had not spoken since the day of the fight, but now he seemed drawn to them the way a fly is drawn to jam.

One evening he brought a bag of clothes to sell and accepted so low a price that even Muhlis was suspicious.

"What does he want?"

"I suppose he wants to come on the picnic," said Mehmet.

"Really? Not him!" Muhlis was sceptical.

"He does," said Mehmet. "He's the sort of person who can't miss anything."

"Why doesn't he ask, then?"

"He's afraid we'll say no."

"You don't want to ask him, do you?" Muhlis's face was mocking.

"No . . ."

"What's the matter, then?"

"I don't know. . . ." He really didn't know what was wrong. He just had a bad feeling. There was something threatening about Hakan. His family was the kind who doesn't give anything away: they'd sell their toenails, if they got a chance.

"Forget it," said Muhlis, and he spat expertly after Hakan's fat, receding back.

Sunday morning was misty and cool. They gathered early and harnessed Yıldız to the painted cart. They helped Muhlis climb up and sat Filiz beside him. Muhlis clicked his tongue, Yıldız put down her head, and the cart wheels squeaked and then rolled easily over the plain. They talked quietly. Mehmet was especially quiet. He was

141

thinking of Hayri and of how much he would have liked him to be there, how he would have talked and told them stories, stories of the heroes of long ago who had passed over this plain. Korsan, loping in great sweeping circles, was following all the new scents. Then Mehmet, waiting for him to catch up, heard laughter. He turned, and there in a giggling, creeping bunch were the children. There must have been twenty, each carrying a bundle or plastic bag. Now, delighted to be discovered, they started to run toward the cart.

"Look, we've caught you! You couldn't trick us!" they shouted. They raced on and surrounded Yıldız, fluttering up and down, mocking the big ones for not seeing them and begging to be lifted up onto the cart. Korsan came bounding back and leaped around them as though he were a young dog again. Muhlis had been right: animals need holidays, too.

A single figure stood and watched them go. It was Hakan. He was carrying a big bag of food and bottles of lemonade. He knew the picnic was going to be today: he had cornered one of the little children and pinched him a bit and got the truth out of him. But at the last minute his courage had failed him, and he had hung back, and now he settled down on the edge of the plain to eat all the fine food that he had not really wanted to share anyway. His jealousy hurt like a pain in his stomach.

They made their way over the plain to the place where the willows and hazel trees were growing out of the edge of the pool. It wasn't even a big pool, but it held enough water to grow those trees and to lie cool and clear under their rustling leaves. At one time, perhaps when the pond had been swollen by the melting snows, its waters had swirled round and round and had washed away the banks of earth and uncovered a tiny beach of gray stones. At the end of the summer there was not much water in the streambed, but it was enough to edge the banks with green grasses and to scatter the reds and golds of wild-flowers among them.

"I could paint that," said Muhlis, looking around carefully. They spread their rugs on the stones, and Ayşe and Elif put the food in the shade. Mehmet walked along the bank with Korsan at his heels. Perhaps if you walked on, you could follow this stream to a big river and then on again to the sea. Hayri would have known. He would have liked it here. It was hot, even in the shade. The flowers of the chicory plant, which would have been bright blue in the early morning, were already losing their color. They were fading to a pale gray beneath the sun. You could almost smell the sun on the earth.

Mehmet kicked off his shoes and lay down on the edge of the stream, trailing his fingers in the water. The voices of the other children seemed far away. Some had begun a game of soccer . . . that was Freckles yelling . . . he'd stepped on a thistle . . . it was too hot for soccer anyway . . . in the evening maybe. Others were building dams, making tiny rivers and seas among the shallows. Later, when it was cooler, he would teach them how to make water mills, if he could still remember. He heard the *slap, slap* of cloth in running water. Were they washing clothes? He'd helped with that, too, back in the village when he'd been a little boy. He had gone down to the river with Ayşe and Elif, who had slapped and scrubbed

143

and scrubbed until their arms ached and their fingers were blue from the chill of the water. Then they had called to him to stop building his water mill or dam and to come and do something useful. He never had finished a water mill properly, but this afternoon he would.

He could hear the *pop, pop* as the seedpods of the wild clover dried and burst open, shooting their seeds out onto the plain like tiny bullets. He rolled over onto his back and wriggled deeper into the grass. Was that the smell of smoke and the crackle of a flame among dry sticks? Why of course — they'd be making a fire. He could see a beetle moving near his cheek. The brilliant, burning sun had found it deep between the roots and stems and made it shine like a jewel. He could hear laughter — high, helpless laughter: that must be Elif and Ayşe. Then there was Ramazan's deep laughter, as he begged someone to stop, to please stop. Then he heard the delighted chatter of children, tormenting a grown-up. He shut his eyes, just for a minute, because the sun was so bright. The sounds of laughter became quieter and quieter.

Mehmet must have slept a long time. Ayşe was shaking his shoulder. Surely they weren't leaving already? Had he missed the picnic? He rubbed his eyes. Where was everybody? Why was it so quiet?

"Come on, sleepy," said Ayşe. "We can't start without you." Ramazan stood beside her, and his hand was on her shoulder. He realized now that there must be an understanding between them. Did his parents know? He could imagine the arguments and explosions back in the dust and dirt of the shantytown. But here, under the quivering leaves of the hazel trees, everything seemed peaceful and happy.

They had spread the picnic out on a tablecloth, and it looked beautiful. There were dozens of things to eat. Ramazan had brought most of it: fresh bread, spring onions, salty white cheese, and dark green peppers as hot as coals. He had brought watermelons and left them to cool in the stream. Now he split them open with his knife. The red flesh glistened, and the little children picked out the black seeds and crunched them up. Freckles's mother had prepared real *köfte* made with meat and parsley. Mehmet had not expected anything as good as that. With pride on his face, Freckles watched Ayşe and Elif grilling the meatballs over the fire. Some of the children who had not tasted meat for months were crouched down, very close, breathing in the smell of meat grilled over a wood fire. They never took their eyes from the *köfte*. There were little green cucumbers, peeled and sprinkled with salt, and the big tomatoes of late summer, all red and misshapen and bigger than your hand. There were peaches and even pomegranates. Then there were all sorts of exciting things that the children had brought, and Mehmet wondered how many parents would go to their cupboards later in the day and find them empty. There were half-packets of cookies, and little papers of pie, and a piece of salami cut all crooked, as only a child working in haste would have cut it. There was a half-cup of yogurt and a whole bowl of stuffed peppers, which surely must have been somebody else's lunch. But they ate them all the same. Osman had made sweet cakes, remembering his days as a pastry cook. He had made them very early in the morning, and Elif had taken them to the bakery to be baked with the first batch of bread. They ate them and they ate everything and thought it was the nicest meal of their lives.

Afterward some of the boys tried to fish and others played marbles. Korsan, whose wound had almost healed, plunged into the stream to fetch sticks, then shook himself dry in a shower of droplets that sent the children diving for cover. Osman lifted the children onto Yıldız's back, and she trotted out, with Freckles dashing behind with a steadying hand. For a moment the children were fearless riders on their way to victory as Yıldız held her head high like a young horse. Muhlis sat in the shade of a tree and watched her. The children paddled, some wading in deep, others squatting in the shallows looking for pretty stones. The dullest stones looked beautiful when you held them in the water. Elif took off Filiz's dress and let her splash and splash and fall down in the water and cry out that she was swimming, really swimming!

It was the sort of day that should never end, but the shadows were growing longer, and Filiz coughed a little; one or two of the children were half asleep, and others admitted, in the end, that they had not really told their parents where they were going. So they packed up and stamped out the fire, and the children gathered their bunches of wilting flowers, and they made their way back across the dried-up plain.

Then they heard the shots. At first just one, which perhaps only Ramazan and Osman recognized. Then they heard two more, with their echoes, from somewhere among the houses of the shantytown. They had been

146

straggling along the path in groups of twos and threes, but now they drew close together.

"I expect it's a wedding," said Osman, but it didn't sound like one. People fired a whole volley of shots at a wedding. Then a single shot came from their right. They could see a truck moving slowly, followed by a few men. Ramazan began to lift the children onto the cart: everybody knew that these were troubled times, times of quiet revenge on dusky evenings. They walked more quickly and didn't speak. There was the truck, not a big one, a covered truck, really. Two men picked something up from the edge of the plain and tossed it into the back of the truck. The hackles rose up along Korsan's back, and he growled suspiciously.

"I'll go and see what it is," said Ramazan. He started forward, and Mehmet went with him. It was as though the men had been waiting for them. Had they done something that they didn't know about? Korsan ran in front. His big wrinkled head was held to one side, and a warning rumbling came from his throat. A voice that Mehmet knew cried out, "That's him! That's the one I told you about!"

A single shot cracked. Korsan bounded into the air and fell down onto his shoulder. His legs worked as though he were running on, but he didn't move from the ground. There was another shot — and he trembled all over and his mouth opened and he made a tiny, whimpering sound. The man with the shotgun came running out from behind the truck, shouting and excited.

"Stay there, children! Don't go near it!"

They froze, too startled even to cry. The man gave

147

Korsan a cautious prod with his foot and called again, proudly.

"Did you see that? A single shot? You got off lightly. We've been out looking for that dog all day."

"In the name of God, what have you done, you fool?" Ramazan looked tall and dark, and the man stepped back.

"Now, look here, I'm only doing my job. That dog's got rabies. Didn't you know that? We've been right through your district, on orders from the mayor himself. There's rabies here. I was told particularly to watch out for this dog. A Kangal, isn't he?"

"Who told you?" But Mehmet knew before he asked.

"Why, that boy who's been here, helping us," said the man and turned around to point, but the boy was, of course, no longer there.

"You've killed my dog." Mehmet could hear the children on the cart begin to cry in small, frightened hiccups.

"It doesn't matter to me whose dog it is. Dogs without a number have to be shot — shot or poisoned. Those are my orders. I'm not keen on shooting where there's a crowd of people, but with a big dog like that I wasn't sure how much poison I'd need. Besides, I wasn't eager to get too close to a sick dog like that."

"He wasn't sick."

"That's what you say, but I had information to the contrary. I can't see no number, not in this light." He was a little gingery man, with broken yellow teeth, a patchy moustache, and small woman's hands. Mehmet knelt down and felt in the familiar soft fur. He found the tag.

"You made a mistake."

148

The man stroked his moustache and ran his tongue over his crooked teeth.

"It's too late now." He gave Korsan another kick with his foot. "You should have been more careful — could have been a valuable dog, that."

··{ 10 }··

MEHMET watched the other boys setting off for school. There were Freckles and the other soccer players looking very different in white shirts and jackets and ties. They stopped at his house and called up to the window.

"Come on, it's not too late — you registered after all. . . ." That was Freckles.

"We'll wait. Get your things together," urged another, and for a moment Mehmet was envious. It could be fun in school, apart from the lessons: you belonged to a school, and it gave a shape to the days and months. They were still waiting for him. Why not go? It wasn't his fault that his parents were so stupid and did not have the courage to stand up to Yusuf Amca. Why should he have to help them out? He could go back to school and work part-time. Lots of the boys did that. He could move in with Muhlis; they'd talked about it often enough. Here he was a worm — a worm, just like his parents, who didn't even wriggle when people walked all over them. That's what Ramazan said: if you act like a worm, of course people walk on you, but nobody treads on a scorpion if they can help it.

A big crowd of boys and girls had gathered outside the house. Every family in the shantytown knew about the killing of Korsan. They had all said it was a shame and a disgrace, but none of them had had the courage to con-tradict Hakan. They could have told the marksman that Korsan was a healthy dog, well known to them and that he had been inoculated against rabies. But they hadn't. Living in the shantytown makes one as cautious and care-ful as a rat in the shadows. You don't look for trouble, not these days. And hadn't they all heard the stories of Korsan being lost and returning injured in the company of a boy who was either mad or sick or both? One could never be sure of anything. That dog might, after all, have been sick. They had remained quiet. They had kept their children close and watched with horrified fascination as the men went through the neighborhood poisoning and then shooting all the dogs and cats they could find. It wasn't for them to protest, they had said, and they had hidden their own pets, many of whom had not been inoculated. These, they had said, were different.

Hakan had offered to help the men, saying that he knew the district well. He knew the hideouts of lots of animals, he said, especially where the late summer litters of puppies and kittens ran about in the sun. It had been a nasty day's work, but Hakan had licked an ice cream as he watched the poisonings and had asked when the shooting would begin. The men had explained that they

151

were to shoot only an animal that they suspected might be dangerous or that they couldn't reach with poison. There was always a danger of bullets ricocheting in these crowded districts and then people who'd left their children out on the streets made an awful fuss if one got hit. No, poison was good if the animal wasn't too big.

Then Hakan had told them about Korsan. He hadn't meant to at first, but once he'd started, he just went on. He told them how Korsan had been newly brought from the country and how he probably had not been inoculated. He told them how he'd been running with a pack of wild dogs and how the boy he'd been with had gone mad. It made a good story. Hakan believed it himself when he had finished. He had offered to show them where Korsan was and they had agreed.

Now that it was too late, the people were sorry. A feeling of sympathy for Mehmet, mixed with a feeling of guilt, had made them tell their children to stop by on the way to school and see if they couldn't persuade him to go with them. It was a shame, they said.

It was too late. It was no good pretending that it wasn't. He shook his head at them. No, he wasn't going back to school. Korsan was dead. And so was that whole way of life — of stealing summer days for play, out on the plains — that was dead, too. He shook his head again. No, he couldn't go to school any longer, and besides, he had other things that he must do. They hung around, then looked at the time and reluctantly went away. Mehmet leaned on the windowsill, watching. He saw a single figure start down the path, too; it kept a careful distance between itself and the others. Freckles, turning back to wave to Mehmet, caught sight of Hakan. He crouched down on all fours and pretended to run around barking. Hakan paused and fiddled with his shoelaces. Then the boys howled and barked and bayed and growled. Women and children came to their doorways to watch, and as the boys barked and barked, Hakan slunk away to get to school by another road.

The house was quiet. The younger children were playing outside. His mother had gone to work, too. His grandparents were the only people in the house, and they were busy on either side of the window. His grandmother was sewing buttons on a pile of shirts that Yusuf had brought. His grandfather was folding the shirts and sliding them into plastic bags with Yusuf's name on the outside. SENSITIVE PEOPLE CHOOSE YUSUF CLOTHING was what each label said. His grandmother held the cloth very close to her face and stitched and stitched. Her weather-beaten forehead was all creased up with worry. They had finished several, but the remaining pile was big. Everybody was working except for him. No, his family wasn't stupid or lazy. No, he didn't think that of them, but it was just that they had lost all their courage. This awful, unending fight for a little more money, this fight ate them up like some terrible disease. He did not want to catch it, yet he knew he had to work. He could have joined Ramazan and Muhlis; he knew they were going out buying today, but he also knew that they would insist on sharing their earnings, and he wouldn't really have earned his share. It would also postpone the trip that he knew he must make: he must go and see Hayri and tell him that Korsan was dead. Ayşe and Ramazan had offered to go with him but he wanted to go alone. Hayri was his friend. It was they who had shared that which had been killed out there on the plain.

Zekiye Hanım led Mehmet up to Hayri's room. Hayri was sitting up in bed surrounded by a pile of books. He was so engrossed in his reading that he didn't notice Mehmet come in. He looked stronger already, and if it hadn't been for the fading sores and bruises, one would not have thought there was much wrong with him. Zekiye Hanım had said that he could hear much more clearly now and that the harsh, uneven sound to his voice had gone. Mehmet could hardly believe that anyone could change so much. Zekiye Hanım left them alone, and Mehmet began his story. It was easier to tell Hayri than Mehmet had expected. Hayri didn't cry or curse or protest. He just listened and turned the pages of the book he was reading. Then he shrugged and said with a sad half laugh, "Poor old Korsan. So he caught it, too, did he? It doesn't pay to play the hero."

"I'm sorry; it's all my fault."

"No, I guess it had to be." He poured himself a glass of *ayran* from a jug beside the bed, and flipped over the pages as though he didn't want to forget his place. Mehmet could not believe that it was Korsan they were talking about. Had Hayri truly heard?

"It didn't have to be! How can you say that?"

Mehmet forgot that his friend was still sick and weak. "It didn't have to be. If I hadn't brought him, he'd still be alive, back in the village. He'd be alive and happy, and we could have gone back and seen him. It's all my fault — and it's Hakan's fault, and it's my parents' fault: if they

154

weren't so mixed up with my uncle and aunt, I wouldn't have had all these quarrels with Hakan, don't you see, Hayri? It needn't have happened. If things had been different, only a bit different . . ." He was the one crying now — he was the one who couldn't bear it.

"But things aren't different."

"They should be different." Mehmet wiped his eyes on his shirtsleeve.

"That's another matter," said Hayri, grinning, as though he enjoyed the problem. "I've talked to Ahmet Bey and Zekiye Hanım a lot. Wanting things to be different and pretending that they are, that's another matter altogether."

"I don't understand," muttered Mehmet. It sounded like being clever with words to him. It was the sort of thing that teachers did sometimes — being clever, with nothing to show for it except that you felt foolish at the end. It was too complicated for him. He knew one thing: Korsan was dead and he need not have died. And he knew something else: that he and Hayri could never now be the friends that they had been. It was not only Hayri who had traveled away from their childhood in the village. Mehmet had, too. He had found within himself a capacity for rage and anger at the way things were that made him feel much, much older. He couldn't say it, though, not to Hayri. So all he said was, "If I'd left Korsan with the teacher like they told me to, he'd still be alive."

"Maybe," murmured Hayri indifferently, "but it doesn't matter now."

"Doesn't matter?"

"I didn't say that. I said it doesn't matter *now*." Hayri

155

looked tired, and his voice was tired, too. "It's no good dreaming . . . of anything. That's what we've all been doing; my teacher dreamed of making me a great student." He sat up, gripping the edge of the *yorgan*, and spoke excitedly. "My parents dreamed of having a famous son. And I dreamed, too. Don't you remember how I dreamed of going to America? Well, we came here, and I studied. I won that scholarship. I knew I would. I hardly had to study for it. My name was in the paper, my father took me to register at that famous school, and, do you know, we couldn't pay. I'd won the place, but my father couldn't pay, and so I couldn't go and they gave the place to somebody whose father could pay. And my father said to me, 'Don't tell your mother.' He thought it was a shame on the family. He said the shame would kill her, so I didn't tell her. We went home, and he said that he had registered me. I could see that it was *him* that it was killing. One day went by and then two days, and on the third day he said he couldn't breathe, and he went outside, and he died right there. The last thing he said to me was, 'Don't tell her.'"

"Did you?"

"No. After we'd buried him, she went out and bought me a shirt and a jacket for school. I went in the morning and I came back in the evening, just as if I were in school."

"Didn't she realize?"

"No, but you know what my mother was like." Mehmet nodded. She was a country woman, even though she was as pale and thin as bleached wood. She

156

would have believed that stones could float if you told her.

"No, she didn't know about me. She only knew she was ill. That was what *I* didn't know. When the neighbors took her to the hospital, the doctors said it was much too late to save her, and too expensive to treat her, so she died. Do you know what I did then? I pretended to myself that I really was going to school. Even when they turned me out of the house, I kept on studying. I went and lived in the streets, and I kept on studying."

"That was in the cinema?"

"Yes. All the time I pretended that things weren't like what they really are. Ahmet Bey says that that is what makes you mad. He says that it breaks you apart, like it nearly did me."

"And now?"

"Now, I know that even if I can never go back to that school, I can go to another school when I'm well again. Zekiye Hanım wants me to stay here and live with her."

"Will you do that?"

"Yes, it suits me here."

"I suppose it would," said Mehmet. Hadn't Hayri always been a special person? Hadn't his poor father who'd died of a broken heart, called him a "strained" child? For Hayri there ought to be a happy end — the world could not be that bad. For him, who wasn't special and for whom no one had sewn a prayer into a bag to keep him safe, there seemed to be no escape from the storm except to bend a bit lower. Nobody had offered him a home. Nobody had even offered to take away his guilt.

He was happy for Hayri, but he longed for someone to say, "It wasn't your fault, Mehmet." It did not have to be true, but he wanted somebody to say those words.

The days passed, and still Mehmet found no work. His family made no comment. Maybe they were trying to be kind, but to Mehmet it felt like indifference. They didn't care enough to ask, and on top of everything, the only thing they talked about was Elif's curtains. He didn't understand it. Family chatter, it seemed to him, especially women's chatter, was either embarrassing or stupid; either way he didn't want to listen. When they got on to illnesses and births and knitting patterns, he usually left. Only an idiot like Hakan could take that sort of thing. Now here was his whole family talking about curtains. Elif had bought them — green velvet curtains that were to hang from floor to ceiling in her matchbox of a house. It was beautiful material, and when she had sewn them, they would be the envy of everybody. Even Fatma Teyze didn't have anything so fine. Mehmet didn't see what all the fuss was about. Hadn't Ayşe cut off her hair to buy medicines and clean sheets for Muhlis? They had made a lot of fuss over that, but this seemed to be different. They couldn't stop talking about it. Even his grandfather, who was the most understanding person in the world, did not approve of the new curtains.

"Fine feathers don't make a peacock," he said, and Elif's cheeks paled with disappointment and anger.

"Why shouldn't I have pretty things?" She folded up the material sullenly, with her lips pressed together and her chin stuck out.

"But how will you pay for it?" asked Mehmet's mother worriedly.

"I haven't got to pay for it . . . well, not now."

"Whatever do you mean?"

"Well, I haven't got to pay all at once." They weren't going to turn all her pride and joy to ashes. "I pay by installments every week. Our landlady showed me how to do it. Everybody pays like that."

"Surely there were things you needed more," suggested Ayşe gently.

"You can talk!" spat Elif, and they were the first unkind words Mehmet had ever heard her speak to Ayşe. "Who bought things for that gypsy and for his brother?"

There was a thick silence in that close room.

"She didn't mean that," said Osman nervously, trying to break the silence. He hated disputes; he would do anything for peace. He had agreed to buy the curtains for the sake of peace. It was the only thing you could hope for — a little peace at home — it did not seem much to pay for the return of Elif's sparkling laugh and tender touch. He had never imagined that such a thing as curtains could turn everyone against his wife.

"It's important to her," he said, watching Elif's trembling fingers with their little pink nails trying too hastily to ram the cloth back into its package. Little Filiz coughed and went from one to the other of them, wanting to climb into somebody's arms, but they didn't notice her. Mehmet drew her onto his lap and kissed her; he knew how she felt. He was surprised how hot her forehead was. He would have told Elif, if it had not seemed like trouble making to say it just then. They'd grumble at her for that,

159

too. It didn't seem fair. They were busy giving their own lives a different pattern. He couldn't see why Elif couldn't do what she liked. If she liked pretty things, why shouldn't she have them?

Mehmet began to come home less and less often. He spent most of his time with Muhlis. Ramazan's leave was over, and as the season changed, Muhlis said that they should do as much business as they could before snow and mud closed the roads.

"Does the snow get so deep?"

"It's not so much the snow as the mud," explained Muhlis. "I'm always afraid Yıldız will slip again in the mud. Anyway, people don't like to open their doors in cold weather, and they certainly don't want to stand around selling things. I don't go out so much in the bad weather: once you've got your clothes soaked through, it isn't so easy to dry them. Though it shouldn't be as bad this year." He patted the stove.

Throughout November and December, Muhlis and Mehmet continued to go to Zekiye Hanım's house. They swept up the leaves and cut down the plants before the coming winter, but it was clear that there was not going to be much more work until the spring. The grass hardly grew on these short, cold days, and the soil had become as sticky as glue with the onset of the rains. On their last visit they split and stacked half a cord of wood. It was hard work, and Mehmet labored without stopping. He spotted Hayri's shadow behind the curtains in the living room. Now there was more than the curtains separating them. Hayri had joined a world beyond the reach of

Mehmet and Muhlis. He had slipped as easily into it as a lizard on a sun-warmed wall slips into a crack. He was back in school. Once Mehmet had seen him going down the road in the center of a crowd of boys from Zekiye Hanım's neighborhood. He had been telling them something, and they had been close to him, as quiet as mice, and then they burst out laughing and hung on each other's shoulders and slapped Hayri on the back. Then they had crowded around him again, begging for another story. Mehmet had kept down behind the wall. He had been pruning the roses before piling straw over them. The winter would be long and cold — four or five months of frosts, Zekiye Hanım had said. If the plants were not protected, they would freeze. It was like preparing the garden for a threatening war, except that it was somebody else's country that he was making ready to withstand the siege. Hayri would be inside these stone walls, whereas he would be outside, where gusts of freezing wind blew the dead leaves into the mud. Mehmet brought the ax down with such force that the log splintered; the two halves sprang apart, and the blade sank down into the block.

Just when he had given up hope, he found a job. He was coming down from the old city after doing business with the secondhand clothes dealer. It was pouring rain, and the streets were running with mud. The dust of summer had turned into a thick, dark, oily paste. He was spattered with it, right up to his knees. The more it rained, the more mud there seemed to be. He had made a good deal of money with the clothes, and he felt so satisfied that he stopped to give a bill to a beggar. The man crouched on

161

the pavement, with his cut-off stumps of legs gleaming white and smooth in the pelting rain. Mehmet was glad there was only a short line for the *dolmuş*. The soles of his shoes had holes, and his feet ached from the cold.

But as the *dolmuş* began to pull out of the *dolmuş* park, its wheels spun wildly, spitting out mud. The vehicle couldn't move. The driver cursed. Mehmet, who was sitting in the front, offered to get out in the pouring rain and push. He pulled out the thickly folded newspapers that he kept under his jacket against the cold and slipped them under the spinning wheels. Then he pushed with all his power. His strength surprised him. The wheels gripped, and the *dolmuş* eased up the slope. Mehmet ran after it and jumped in while it was still moving.

The rain was coming down more heavily; the driver jerked his head from side to side, trying to see. Mehmet picked up a cloth and wiped the inside of the windshield clean. The driver told him to collect the fares. He did so easily — bargaining with Muhlis had made him clear-headed about money. When they reached Şentepe, the driver turned to him. "You're the boy that had that dog, aren't you?"

"Yes."

"You not in school?"

"Not now. I'm looking for work."

"You want to work with me, collecting the fares, minding the *dolmuş*, that sort of thing?"

"All right."

"I had a boy, but he cheated on the money."

"I won't do that."

"You'd better not. If you do I'll break every bone in your body."

"I told you, I'm not a thief."

That was how it happened: in two minutes he had a job.

It was good to be working. Once again the day had a shape. It started in the dark. At six in the morning Mehmet had to be at the *dolmuş* stop in Şentepe for the first run of the day. They worked on until Huseyin, the driver, passed the bus over to his brother in the evening. This brother, Hasan, drove until the early hours of the morning, and if Hasan's boy didn't show up, Mehmet stayed on. Often he didn't bother to go home at all. He wrapped himself in a blanket and stretched out on the backseat. Huseyin, for all his unshaven face and loud voice, was nicer than he looked. At the end of the week he paid Mehmet, and fairly, and took him to lunch in a workman's restaurant. The meal, which consisted of dried beans and chocolate pudding with pistachios sprinkled on top, made Mehmet feel good, but it was nothing like the good feeling he had when he handed his first wages to his father.

"Well, well," said his father. "Didn't I tell you that you'd find something? It's a good job, a *dolmuş* driver. I knew my son would manage. You've got the makings of a businessman. Before we can blink, you'll have your own *dolmuş*." He had his foolish, dreaming eyes on the little bundle of bills in Mehmet's hand. Mehmet passed the money to his mother, and his father moistened his lips with the tip of his tongue. His mother looked anxiously from her husband to her son.

"It's for the rent," said Mehmet firmly.

"Why, of course it's for the rent." His father smiled regretfully. "Whatever did you think?"

It grew colder and colder. Huseyin told Mehmet not to sleep in the bus or he'd freeze to death. Mehmet didn't believe him. Then, very early one morning, when it was so cold it almost hurt to draw a breath, Mehmet rested a careless hand on the *dolmuş* door and felt his flesh stick. He pulled away in panic and felt a burning on his finger pads as the soft skin tore off.

"That'll teach you," said Huseyin roughly, and it did.

Winter dragged on, and the streets were covered with a dangerous mixture of ice and mud. It snowed heavily. They carried bags of sand and grit to help them over the ice, but as it was, Mehmet often had to get down and push. He didn't mind; he hadn't known he was so strong. They saw many accidents along the road, but Huseyin was a careful driver despite all his cursing and shouting. Mehmet was glad to be out of the house, where it was so bitterly cold. It might stink of cigarettes and wet boots in the *dolmuş*, but at least it was warm and Huseyin had a supply of tapes that he played loudly and endlessly as they drove up and down the winding road.

Muhlis had taken Yıldız into his house with him. He said that the roads were too dangerous for her. On better days he went out himself on foot. In their district everyone was wearing their clothes layer upon layer, so they had nothing to sell. He had to walk far afield to the better

164

areas, and even then business was not good. Sometimes he went through the garbage bins looking for tin cans and bottles, and Mehmet would see him from the *dolmuş*, bent double under a huge bag. But he mainly stayed at home with Yıldız. He reminded Mehmet of an animal crouching in his cave and waiting for the coming of spring with a patience that Mehmet did not have. Muhlis could sleep for hours, sometimes it seemed for days; he'd turn over and say something and then go back to sleep again. Mehmet visited him most evenings, and they often toasted bread on top of the stove for their supper, but he found the closeness of the little house overpowering. He couldn't stay long; he was filled with energy, he was restless, and the tiny house was like a prison.

That winter pneumonia stalked through the shantytown. Like a wolf coming out of the dark places in the forest to hurl itself upon the faltering lamb, it searched for the child who was weakened by the long winter of hardship. Elif's little girl still coughed. She coughed so much that they had all got used to it. Children coughed in winter, and when spring came, they would get better. That's what they said. Weren't her cheeks red? Red cheeks are a sign of health.

"I'm worried," confessed Elif. She had come on a rare visit to Mehmet's mother and father. The affair of the green curtains had spoiled their former happy relationship.

"Well, take her to a doctor. We're in the city now. And your husband has a job," said his father harshly.

"Yes. Yes, I could." Elif was trembling. Mehmet remembered the bright-eyed wild birds that he and Hayri had trapped back in the village. They had fluttered help-lessly against the bars of the cage, seeking a way out that was not there. They had always kept the doors of the cage firmly shut.

"Or take her into one of the hospitals in the city, after all, you seem to know your way there. You got those curtains, didn't you?" That was his mother, made cruel or thoughtless or both. He didn't know which, and he didn't like it. Now that he was older, he wouldn't shut anything up in a cage — not ever. He couldn't understand why his family didn't see the fear in Elif's face. She was asking for help, and they wouldn't give it because once she had been foolish. He smoothed out the curls on Filiz's head. Her hair was damp, and she burned with fever. She was so quiet you might have thought she was asleep.

"If you ask me," said Mehmet's father, "I can't see anything wrong with her now. Last month you complained that she kept you awake all night coughing, and now that she's quiet, you're still complaining. You young people, you're never satisfied." Elif did not reply. Getting ready to leave, she wrapped Filiz in a blanket; neither of them had a winter coat. Mehmet followed her down the steps.

"I'll go with you to the hospital if you like." He wondered why Osman didn't go. She didn't look at him. "Do you need some money?"

"Of course not." She hurried away in her plastic slippers over the hard, frozen snow.

Suddenly the weather became milder, and for several days the sun broke through the cloud of smoke that hung

166

over the city. People came out and chatted with their neighbors. Mehmet's mother saw Elif in the bazaar and gave them the news that Filiz was so much better that Elif had bathed her before the coming *bayram*.

"What did I tell you?" said Mehmet's father.

Early one morning, there were only a few people waiting for the *dolmuş*. They were the regulars, and they greeted Mehmet by name. It was noticeably warmer, and for the first time they could have the window down. They were just setting off when one of the passengers told Huseyin to wait. Another passenger was coming. It was a woman with a green shawl thrown over her pajamas. The men moved seats so that she might sit by herself. Then they heard her sobbing cries and they flung the door open. It was Elif with Filiz wrapped in a blanket in her arms.

"For the love of God, take me to the hospital!" she cried. One shouted that the nearest hospital was in Ulus; another said that it would be best to stop at a doctor. Huseyin began to drive dangerously fast. Elif couldn't tell them what the matter was but hugged the child tightly to her. Her face was no longer pretty, and her terrified eyes did not see Mehmet. They passed the *dolmuş* stops without halting, but a red light made them finally stop. Huseyin leaned back and turned the blanket down from Filiz's face. The lights changed, and all the cars began to honk at them. He lifted the little hand, and they all saw how it fell back.

"She's not dead," breathed Elif. "She can't be dead because she was alive. She was alive when I left home. I know she was. . . ."

The men looked, all of them, and Mehmet, too. The child was still warm inside her blankets, but as they bent over her, the dark eyes never moved.

It was strange what things people said after Filiz's death. Mehmet expected Yusuf Amca to say things like "It's the will of God" and "God gives and God takes." It went with his fancy, polished shoes and his stomach that bulged so prosperously out of his vest. It went with his tone of voice. He expected Fatma Teyze to come hundreds of times for tea and tears; of course she would say things about "young women who did not do their duty as mothers." People like them talked like that. He expected it. But Mehmet did not expect his own family to act the way they did. His mother said that poor Filiz was better off dead. His father said that since Elif was so young, they could have many more children. Even his grandmother, pressed up against the window to catch the last light for her button sewing — even she stroked Elif's hand and said that she shouldn't be sad — her next baby would be a boy, a fine strong boy, who would be as handsome as his father! Osman wasn't much better: he smiled wryly, smoothed his moustache, and stretched out a slim, straight leg and tried to catch Elif's eye.

Elif didn't say a thing. She sat in a corner and covered her mouth with the edge of her scarf. It was a big white sheet of a scarf, not a pretty embroidered one. She kept fiddling with it, pulling it farther down her forehead, so that they could see only her eyes. It dragged around her and hid her pretty neck and arms, and Mehmet thought again of those birds. In the end they had stopped fluttering against the bars and had settled on the floor, with their heads sunk down into their puffed-out feathers and their little eyes hooded. He and Hayri had thought then that they had tamed them.

Yes, it was very strange. Nobody seemed to think about Filiz. Nobody asked whether she had wanted to be buried down in the cold winter earth. Nobody seemed to burn with anger as he did. They drank their tea and wept and remembered other children who had died. That was the trouble with all of them. They knew everything there was to know about dying. They were expert in dying and they knew how to bury their dead and they knew how to mourn. Mehmet was revolted to hear Fatma Teyze discussing recipes for making the sherbet to be offered to the guests at the *Mevlut*, the prayers that would be held forty days after Filiz's death. She, who had not made that child a cup of tea while she was alive, was worried about whether the sherbet should be flavored with rose-water or lemon.

"Lemon," said Osman, in a tone that said he was grateful to Fatma Hanım for asking. Mehmet was impatient and restless. He got up and left the room. They knew how to die. They knew a million ways to die, but they did not know how to live.

·{11}·

MUHLIS was sitting in front of his house painting his cart. He had redone the waterfalls and flowers and was now working on the hubs of the wheels. They were the only unpainted parts. Mehmet squatted down beside him. The sun was warm on the back of his neck. It was spring again. The soccer players were out — he would join them later. Muhlis said he might join in, too. His foot didn't hurt anymore, though it flopped a bit. He thought he must have cut through something more than just skin. Still, it was all right. But before he did anything, he was going to finish the picture first. He had planned most of it out during the long winter. It was a circle of children holding hands, with their feet coming together at the center of the wheel. One child was much smaller than the rest. Mehmet could see that it was Filiz, though why, he was not sure. There she was in her flowery dress over red pajamas, and smiling, too. It was beautiful, and Muhlis painted with a swift, confident hand. When

170

Mehmet had tried to paint or draw in school, he had always done more erasing than drawing. Sometimes he had rubbed right through a page. His pictures were never as good as he hoped. But Muhlis knew what he was doing. He painted the last blue stripe on a child's green dress, then he stood back and looked at it, satisfied.

It was a good soccer game. Mehmet, standing with the others for the first time since the autumn, found that he was almost the tallest. He would not have thought that crouching in a *dolmuş* all day would have made him grow, but it seemed that it had. He decided that he would buy himself a pair of blue jeans; he'd keep some money back out of his next wages. He might not wear the jeans to work, but on Sundays, like this one, he would wear a new pair of jeans and a new shirt. Then he could go down and see Hayri. He had not been once during the winter months. When he went it would not be to work in Zekiye Hanım's garden; it would be a visit from one friend to another. Muhlis could take the cart. He had repaired it and had replaced some of the heavy old boards with light ones. He was eager to try it out. Everybody admired the paintings, and Mehmet knew that Muhlis wanted to show them to Zekiye Hanım. There was one other figure in that ring of children that caught Mehmet's attention: it was a tall, thin girl. She had slanting eyes — slanting like Muhlis's own eyes. She wore gold bracelets on her wrist, and gold coins hung round her neck. When the wheel turned, the gold paint sparkled in the sun.

It rained on the morning of the proposed trip, and the roads were muddy.

171

"The cart will get dirty," said Mehmet. He pointed to the girl with the gold bracelets and said lightly, "Look, your bride will get mud on her."

"She already has."

"Where?" Mehmet bent down to look. Her paint glistened and shone. He rubbed his sleeve over the picture. It was nicer than a lot of postcards that you saw.

"She's not my bride, anyway — she's my sister."

"Your sister? What sister?"

"You know, the one I told you about."

"Oh, that one." He looked again at the picture. Yes, of course, the girl was like Muhlis.

"I mean to say," said Muhlis, buckling Yıldız into the shafts, "she didn't ask to be done in, no more than your niece did."

"Is she dead then?"

"No, not her — she's a tough one, like me."

"Why is she done in then?"

"Well, you saw her, didn't you? You know, that day when we went up to the castle."

"She was the girl in that old house?"

"That's her."

"What's she doing there?"

"I don't know what she's doing there. You ask too many questions. It doesn't do any good to ask questions."

He remembered the woman's white arm with the little red fingernails, in the shadowy street.

"I mean," said Muhlis, "there should be a place for people like her, like there should be a place for Filiz, and if nobody else will give them a place, why shouldn't I?"

172

He laughed. "Give me a horse, any day." He clicked his tongue, and they were off.

"Have you ever seen a horse with a foal?"

"Yes, of course."

"The coal man said that Yıldız had had a foal, but that was before we got her. A little black foal. I wouldn't have separated them; I'd have kept them together. I'd never sell off a foal as soon as it could pull a cart, the way he did. I often wonder what happened to that foal."

Mehmet recalled the horses back in the village, the pretty mares running with their foals. Without thinking, he said, "We could go back. . . ."

"Go back where?"

"Back to my village."

"I don't want to go back to your village. I starved in my village. Last winter was nothing like the winters in my village. There, it was always winter!"

"I didn't know it was like that."

"Well, it was. Until Ramazan and I came here to Ankara, I had not even seen oranges."

"My village wasn't like that. I mean, we had spring in our village." Mehmet remembered it very clearly. "It was everywhere, not like here, where it's only spring where there's enough water." He pointed to the garden behind the wall. It was not in full leaf yet, but it was coming alive. There were bluebells and hyacinths growing in the shade of the wall. The rosebushes were putting out soft, pointed pink-tipped leaves. The jasmine was blooming and falling over the balconies in a shower of golden flowers. They smelled it as they went through the gate. Mehmet

173

remembered the apple trees back home. This year they would be blooming with no one to see them. No one would have limed their trunks this year. In the autumn, no one would pick the apples; they would fall to the ground and rot there, with only the drowsy bees knowing it.

"You might not like it, but I bet Yıldız would."

If Mehmet had grown, Hayri had grown even taller, so perhaps it wasn't working in a *dolmuş* that made you grow. Hayri was tall and fair, not as fair as he had been as a little boy, but still fair. He was absolutely clean in the way that only people who wash every day in hot water can be clean. He took them into the shady, book-lined room and then brought them drinks on a silver tray. Mehmet, taking his glass, saw his own, black-nailed fingers beside Hayri's. He felt uncomfortable. Why had they come? Hayri talked of his studies. He had been promoted in school: he was with boys two years older than he was. He planned to take another scholarship exam in the summer.

"Do you think you'll pass?" asked Mehmet.

"Yes, if they mark the papers fairly. That's what Ahmet Bey says."

"Then what will you do?"

"Zekiye Hanım thinks I should go away to America."

"That's what you always wanted to do, wasn't it?" Mehmet tried to look interested. Muhlis was not even trying. He had not touched his drink and stared fixedly at a picture of flowers in a vase on the opposite wall.

"Well," said Hayri, "I always wanted to study history, but at school they say I should do math. Math is fun, too,

174

and history has its problems. With history, you're tied down. All the paths bring you back to the present, and I don't like that."

"You're right there," said Muhlis unexpectedly. Mehmet didn't understand; he didn't understand anything, except that he and Hayri were separated as finally as if the wide ocean already lay between them.

"I'm not very enthusiastic about the present," Hayri continued, "but there's not much we can do about it, is there? We can't change things, can we?"

"I can," muttered Mehmet, but too quietly to be heard.

"Since I can't do anything, I might as well go away. I shall go away and never come back. What have I got to come back to? I shall go away and study numbers. It's the sort of thing I like. I feel much happier among numbers. I know exactly what I'm doing, and they are beautiful in a way that history isn't for me, not now, since I came here to Ankara."

"That may be all right for you," said Muhlis. "Numbers can get themselves lost, as far as I'm concerned."

"I know it's all right for me." Hayri sounded regretful. "And I know it's only all right for me because of what Mehmet did. That's what Zekiye Hanım and Ahmet Bey say: if I hadn't had a friend like that, I'd probably be dead now. It's odd — all the time we were kids in the village, I thought I was the one looking after Mehmet. Now, I don't think it was like that. He was the one looking after me all that time."

Mehmet picked at the dirt under his fingernails and looked at the floor. He knew that this was Hayri's way of saying thank you — thank you and good-bye, both at the same time. Hayri was walking away — he had already walked away. He had thrown off his childhood together with the prayer in the bag that he used to wear around his neck. It hadn't done him much good, nor poor Korsan either. He must have forgotten Korsan. He never mentioned him, never asked where he was buried. He must want to forget.

Mehmet didn't want to forget. He didn't like all this forgetting that people did. Numbers indeed — studying numbers . . . He didn't want to lose himself in the beauty of numbers. He wanted to remember.

"I hope you get there," said Mehmet, standing up. "America, I mean. Me, I'm going back to the village."

"I couldn't," said Hayri, as they shook hands. "I'm going away, as far and as fast as I can."

Mehmet and Muhlis went down the marble steps and closed the gate on the scented coolness of the garden.

"Did you mean it, about going to the village?" asked Muhlis, breaking the long silence as they ambled back.

"I think so."

"And did you mean it, about Yıldız liking it there?"

"Why not? There are meadows down by the river, and at this time of year they are full of flowers. Much fuller than Zekiye Hanım's garden. Yıldız would get quite fat. We could let her run with the other horses." He tried to describe to Muhlis the world of his childhood. They could almost see the horses running through the long grass with their manes and tails streaming out; they would be browsing under the apple trees in the evening and in the midday sun they would seek out the shade of the birch wood.

"She might even have another foal next spring," said Muhlis, and he could see her, too, with a little long-legged foal nuzzling under her scarred belly. The foal, with its comic wisp of tail, would always be by her side. If you could paint that, you could paint the finest picture in the world, the sort of picture everyone could understand. "And us?" Muhlis asked.

"I'd go back to school with the other boys in the village. It's a very long walk and you can get frozen if you don't watch out in winter, but it doesn't seem to be so very different here, does it?"

"And me? What about me? I don't remember any old-clothes dealers in my village. We wore our clothes till they rotted, so what will I do?" Mehmet thought for a moment; it was the same in his village. Then he had his wonderful idea.

"You can paint! You can paint pictures and sell them along the road. There are always people going along our main road. They're tourists, going to visit the Hittite ruins — Hayri told me about them. You'd like the ruins; they're older than the castle, I think. Anyway, you could sell your pictures to those tourists."

"I could paint all winter, and in the spring, I could go out and sell. I could sell them off the cart. That wouldn't be hard for Yıldız, pulling a cart of pictures, because once she had her foal, I wouldn't want to work her too hard."

It had started to rain, a spring shower that they hardly noticed. Then it poured down, but they kept on. They had too many plans to make to waste time sheltering from the rain.

"We could get chicks in the spring. I might even get the

177

chickens back from the teacher. And if you've got the time, there are fish in the river."

"I'd have time, wouldn't I?" Muhlis was thoughtful. "I could paint while I was waiting for the fish to bite."

The rain eased off as suddenly as it had begun, and the main road was already drying in patches.

"You could get another puppy," said Muhlis. Mehmet had never thought of that.

"Why not? I could go back to the village where Korsan came from. I could choose one out of a litter." He could almost feel it — feel the softness of its fur and the prick of its tiny milk teeth on his finger as he teased it gently. Some Kangals had blackish faces and muzzles; maybe that would be nice this time.

They turned off the main road. Here the rainwater had deepened the mud. You could not see where the track was. This road was never repaired because it didn't go anywhere important. Actually, you hardly could call it a road. Mehmet felt his old feeling of anger and impatience rising. Look at that: a row of streetlights was on. That was typical, five streetlights swinging above a road on a bright afternoon. Mehmet jumped down into the mud and went ahead. Sometimes the potholes were very deep. It would be a shame to jolt and damage the cart after Muhlis had spent so long repairing it.

He didn't think he would tell his parents that he was going back. He would just leave. He and Muhlis would make secret preparations, and one morning, when his parents bothered to notice that he was not around, he would already be far away. He would tell Ayşe, and she would tell Ramazan. He knew that they exchanged letters in secret. He stepped over a snaking, heavy wire that must have blown down in the storm. Then he jumped over a wide puddle. That was the problem in the village, too. There was water, but not in the right place. Still, you could do something about that, if you wanted to. Perhaps you could really build those dams and water mills that he hadn't been able to finish as a child.

He heard Yıldız. She started a terrible noise that she did not finish, and her brown eyes bulged. She staggered forward, going deeper into the muddy hole. Her legs were shaking and stiff. Then she fell down. She fell down into that frothy pit, and the cart overturned. Muhlis was thrown clear.

"She's caught on that wire!" Muhlis yelled, and he started to claw his way through the mud to her. "It's gone round her legs! I've got to free her!" he cried.

"Don't!" screamed Mehmet. "It's electricity, don't you see?" Yıldız tried to rise once more from the water, and there was blood on her soft lips. "Don't!" Mehmet tried to grab his friend, but Muhlis was quicker. He plunged his arm deep into the water, searching for the wire.

He found it — his shoulders shook and he was flung sideways, and then he rolled over in the water beside Yıldız. The cart's wheel with the pictures of the children spun round and round in the sun — the faces of the children merged and became one as it turned. Then the wheel turned more and more slowly, and the children drew apart, each child alone, though their hands were linked. The girl with the slanting eyes rested her pale cheek close to her brother, and you could not see the sparkle of gold on her wrist, for it lay beneath the water.

Mehmet crawled, then rose unsteadily to his feet. He could barely keep his balance in the oozing mud. He didn't know how long he stood there, looking at them, wiping his hands back and forth on the corner of his jacket. He swallowed and spat and felt that he would never, ever be clean again. People began to gather. A crowd blocked the road, a truck honked and edged forward, and the driver leaned out and looked.

Only after a long time did someone find out how to switch the electricity off. All that time Mehmet just stood there, watching, waiting for Muhlis and Yıldız to move and crawl out. But they didn't. He was cold. He was shaking so that his teeth chattered in the warm sun, and they asked him what had happened, but he couldn't answer. He couldn't say a single word. He rubbed the back of his hand again and again over his mouth, trying to get free from the taste of mud. Women came out, holding their skirts up out of the dirt and telling their frightened children that this was what happened to you if you weren't careful. An official from the council came but didn't even step out of his car. He shook his head and said that it was not his fault. There was almost no helping these people: if you started to mend their roads, they blundered into the trenches, and if you gave them electricity, just look what happened — they killed themselves with it. Mehmet thought he would choke with the unfairness of it all.

"Well," said a policeman, going through Muhlis's pockets, "does anyone know the lad?" They did, in a way, one woman said. He was Muhlis the Thief, but no, not really — it was just a nickname. He was Muhlis the Gypsy, the old-clothes dealer, though, now that she

180

thought about it, nobody knew much about him — it was
other people who said this and that. They were all stony
faced and turned to go. It seemed unfair to repeat gossip,
now that he was dead.

"He has a brother," said Mehmet at last. The policeman, who was kind and sent for a drink of water for him,
wrote everything down. It made about seven lines in his
notebook.

"Nice cart, that," said a man when Yıldız had been cut
free of the traces and the cart righted. He smeared some
of the mud away and laughed at the paintings. Mehmet
could not bear to see his hand on them, fingering the pictures that were all that was left of their dreams. Suddenly
he seemed to wake up from his nightmare, and he
stepped forward. It was his cart, he said, and he had to
take it back. He set himself between the shafts with a rope
around his shoulders, and he flung himself forward with
all the surging energy that he should have used to hold
Muhlis back. He drove himself to the impossible task, and
the cart rolled forward, and the pain in his shoulders,
which seemed as though they must tear off, made him
feel better and alive.

··{ 12 }··

THE NEWS must have traveled before him, because when he finally got home, people watched him from their windows and talked in small groups, nodding toward him. Even Freckles was too busy with something else when Mehmet walked by and didn't look up. Mehmet wished so much that someone would call him over. His family was at home. It was suppertime. They knelt around a pot, set on newspapers on the floor, and were very quiet. They were eating slowly, wiping the last drops of soup from their plates with bits of bread, and they hardly paused. They raised their eyes to him, then went on eating. He could see that they were hungry and did not really want to stop, not even for him. Only Ayşe sat apart, with her face all swollen up with tears and her eyes rimmed in red. He would have liked to run across the room to her, to bury his face in her shoulder and cry into her soft hair. But he didn't. That was now a part of another land, which, it seemed, they had only been visiting. He watched his father pressing his bread onto the drops of soup that had fallen on the newspaper, and then chewing with pleasure. He heard him say, with satisfaction, "Your uncle and aunt were right: I hear that boy has come to a bad end."

"Thank God you weren't on the cart," said his mother, and she tipped the last of the cold soup into a plate and held it out to him. Nobody in the circle moved to make room for him.

"I wish I had been," he said very clearly, not meaning it at all but needing to say it. They looked up at him again, shocked at the words. They whispered prayers and blew over him and said that it was tempting fate to talk like that. Children, it seemed to him, could suffer but must not say so. It also seemed to him that fate did not need tempting. It was crouching, waiting for you on the sunniest of spring days. It sprang at you and got you down by the throat just when you were dreaming of the summer to come. His mother looked at his ruined clothes and offered to get him something clean, but he refused and said that he would go outside to wash.

Ayşe rubbed her eyes and said she would come out with him, and their steps rang together on the half-finished stairs. He told her how it had happened, and she listened, sucking in her bottom lip to stop herself crying.

"I'll write to Ramazan," she said. "I'll tell him what you've told me, how it really was." She spoke so faintly that he had to bend down to hear her. "I shall marry him," she murmured, "when he comes back. And then we'll go away."

"Do they know?" He nodded toward the house.

"I don't think they know anything any longer," she said.

"Where will you go? To Istanbul?" That was the other big city where people went to find work.

"No, no, we'll go away, right away. To another country."

"America?" He thought of Hayri and how he, too, was going.

"Ramazan says we should go to a country called Switzerland. He has a friend in the army who's going there. He says we can come, too. We, we" — she looked away for a moment, biting her lip to try to stop it shaking — "we were going to send for you, for you and Muhlis. We had talked about it. It seemed such a good idea then."

"It's still a good idea, but Muhlis would never have come."

"Why not?"

"He'd never have left Yıldız," said Mehmet, and they almost laughed.

"And you? Would you have come?" Would he? Now that she had asked him, he knew, with certainty, that he did not want to go. To him it felt like being driven away, pushed out of your place in a line. No, he didn't want to go away.

"I thought I'd go back," he said. It sounded stupid, but she didn't seem to think so, because she said that he could take the cart. Then she flushed crimson and looked unhappy because she had forgotten that Yıldız was dead, too.

"Don't worry," he said, and laughed. "I'll be all right. You know what they say: 'A bitter eggplant is not hurt by the frost.'" Then he kissed her good-bye on both cheeks and pretended that it wasn't a real parting. But at the last moment, when he could no longer see her face, he said into the darkness, "I hope you'll be happy with Ramazan."

And she answered, in a voice that was as soft and sure as a dove's, "Oh, I will. I know I will." Then she was gone, back up the track.

It was a warm night. It was as warm as the night when he had first arrived in Şentepe. He remembered waiting out in the dark, being ashamed to enter that bright red room, waiting on and on with the noise of the shanty-town and the scampering of the scavenging dogs. At that time he had been so uncertain of his place that Hakan had knocked him down into the dust. But the past, too, was a distant land, as distant as any Switzerland or America. He crouched down under the tap and pulled off his shirt, then let the water run, streaming all over him. A neighbor came up with a bucket, scolding him that it wasn't clean and that he'd finish the water, but he did not listen. He opened the tap wider still, and the cold water beat down on his face and on his eyelids so that he could not see. He heard her move off, muttering, with the bucket clanking empty against her leg. He cupped his hands and drank and drank, and at last the feel of mud was gone and the pain in his shoulders where the rope had cut into the skin was eased away. When he opened his eyes, there was a little gaggle of giggling boys, watching him curiously and squatting in the mud to dam up the water that he had let run away. He fiddled with the buttons of the shirt and couldn't fasten it, and the children sailed a fleet of egg-

185

shells and onion skins and quarreled about who should be the captain. A year ago, he might have teased them and showed them how to fold a boat from paper; he would have played for a little while, too, but not now. He just stepped over their sea and went on down the track.

There was a single figure leaning against a wall. He knew it was Hakan and that he was waiting for him. He almost turned aside to reach the main road by another path, but then he decided not to. He was not going to turn aside anymore. And besides, it was Muhlis and Ramazan who had always said that everybody should have a chance. He paused long enough for Hakan to take his chance if he cared to.

"My father has a message: you can tell Ramazan that we'll buy that bit of land between the houses, for a good price, considering he doesn't have a deed to it." Mehmet heard him bite into something in the dark. "My mother says that some of your family seem to know where he is, so, you'll tell him, won't you?"

Mehmet heard him rubbing the sole of one of his shoes slowly up and down on the wall behind him. For a moment he thought he was going to hit his cousin. His arm went up and back, and Hakan pressed away against the wall, his foot quite still. Mehmet knew that he could get him down in the mud and tear his clean shirt and knock the food from his hand, but he knew that he would not stop there. By the time that Hakan had shrieked for help and begged him to stop, he would have hurt him, and he didn't want to. He didn't want to even touch him. He stepped up close, so close that he could smell the spiced meat and onions that Hakan turned over in his mouth, and he peered into his eyes and saw the fear there as Hakan turned his head this way and that, messing his neat hair up against the wall and too scared to look Mehmet in the face. They were the eyes of a coward who would never, ever take a chance.

Mehmet smiled at him and made as if he was going to pinch his plump cheek, and he said, "*You* tell him, Fatty." He laughed in his face, and he knew that Muhlis would have been proud of him.

He walked all the way to Zekiye Hanım's house. It must have been after midnight, but a light was still on in the front room. It shone out into the garden and picked out the pale, fluttering wings of silent moths. He slipped inside the walls and breathed again the scents of the spring night. The white jasmine and the fresh mint were almost overpowering as he brushed past them. A few rosebuds were opening, but it was early in the year, and most of them hid among the shining leaves. He bent down and touched the cool shadows between the blades of grass. He stroked his hand over the lawn, and it was as soft as the eyelashes of a child, yet it was not for this he had come. He got to his feet and meant to slip away before anyone could see him. He had no right to be there, and he would have gone had not Zekiye Hanım seen a movement in her garden and come out. When he started to tell her what had happened, he knew why he had come. She would listen and she would hear him. They walked up and down, and she tidied away a trail of jasmine and broke off the dead heads of narcissi, and she listened to everything he had to say and never interrupted. If he had been clever and special, like Hayri, then he could have

187

written it down, but he wasn't. He wasn't even very sure that it was a special story. The policeman had said that things like that were always happening, as though that made it better. At least now, someone else knew, and he was sure that she'd never ever repeat it — not even to Hayri.

"You could, if you wanted to, stay," she said, twisting the shriveled flower heads round and round in her hands. He looked around the garden with its four high walls. He saw the house; in one of the upstairs rooms, Hayri must have been sleeping. The walls were so thick that the snarl of the city reached them only as a murmur with the wind. Once he had wanted to stay. He had envied Hayri his book-lined room.

"You could stay," she said again, "but you don't really want to, do you?"

"No. But thank you. I thought of — well — of going back. We planned to go together, Muhlis and I. We were almost on our way back to the village."

"As far away as that?" she asked. Once, when they had been working in the garden, she had brought out, with the cold water, an atlas, and she had made Mehmet show her where his village was, a tiny black dot on pale green with the brown mountains rising just next to it.

"But we could write, couldn't we, Hayri and I?" He could almost see the mailman coming up the path from the river, going through the birch grove and coming on up, calling that here was yet another letter from Ankara and that he should stir himself and come and get it. Then he saw himself opening it and reading it all alone, and he shivered.

She insisted that he come in, and then she warmed up some food for him. Then, while he ate, she went to her desk in the room where the light still burned, and she took her cash box from a locked drawer and counted into his hands more money than he had ever seen together at one time. He started to say that he could not take it, that they would be furious with him at home, that he couldn't accept gifts, and then he remembered that no one was going to say that to him anymore.

"Come," said Zekiye Hanım, "we can't pretend that you don't need it, and I also can't pretend that I'll miss it." She paused, and he nodded, for of course they both knew that he needed it desperately. "You trusted me with your friend Hayri, didn't you? And now you must trust me again. I'm old enough to know that good people starve just as quickly as bad, and if you ask me, even quicker. Now I'm an old woman, and I don't now expect anyone to listen to me and to my warnings, but you must. I could not let you walk out into a storm a second time, now, could I?"

She closed his fingers firmly around the bills, and then she went with him to the gate and stepped briefly from the shelter of the walls out into the street and watched him set off.

It was just starting to get light when he reached the *dolmuş* park at Ulus. There were few people on the streets, just some men with shovels and axes loitering at the corners, waiting for the hiring of men for daily work to begin. Some still slept against the walls with their caps pulled down over their faces. Others just stood, waiting, with

189

faces as bitter and gray as his father's. Farther up the hill, the stall holders were starting to get the bazaar ready. A small boy, younger than himself, was unloading huge pale cabbages from a truck, and when he set each down, the leaves crunched and squeaked as though they were alive. An old man was smashing up a box and feeding the soft splinters into a hissing fire. Mehmet stopped to warm himself and called over the tea boy. He drank one tea, which was bitter and cloudy, and then another, which was so hot that it burned his mouth. He went on up through the gold market, but here the shops were silent and shuttered. He passed the secondhand clothes shop, and that, too, was shuttered. Yet he hurried, panting for breath as though he had to be somewhere on time. It was stupid, he knew, because he had nowhere to go in the whole city. He had thought he would look at the castle once more, since Muhlis had liked it so much. He could look across the city and out to the plains beyond. As the streets got narrower and steeper, they seemed to press in on him so that he had to stop. He had a stitch in his side.

Somewhere above him a small window opened, and he could smell the old air from a dark, cramped room. He heard sleepy voices and then the sound of water running into a thin tin basin. A cat came down the street with a paper in its mouth. It crouched down in a corner and licked and licked and never took its yellow eyes from Mehmet's face, as though it feared he would snatch the morsel from it. Then a child came out of the house, a little thin girl in pajamas, with her hair sticking up from her face where it had been pressed against the pillow. She didn't see him. He squatted down, waiting. Then the child came back. She carried loaves of bread in her arms and was gnawing at the end of one of them. She glanced at him now, as she stopped at the door, and called shrilly for her mother to open it. Mehmet knew that he had been waiting for the door to open. He called out to the child to wait, and she turned to him with her teeth in the bread and her eyes slanted like two fresh almonds. The door opened a crack, and then wide enough to let the child in. He saw the young woman take the bread from the child and hold it tightly to her. Her nails were as red and as perfect as he had remembered.

"I was a friend of Muhlis," he said, staring at her across the dusty stones of the silent street. Her pale, smooth fingers tightened on the bread. She looked behind her quickly, then, with lips that barely moved, asked what had happened. Mehmet didn't think he could tell her, but he did. She only said, "May God rest his soul in peace," as though nothing in the world could surprise her any longer. She must have been about as old as Ayşe, but Mehmet could never have imagined her skipping in the street. Her slanting eyes in her beautiful face were as worn and shadowy as the stones on the street. Somebody called her from inside the house.

"It's a friend of my brother," she said.

"Then ask them in," called another, pleasantly, and she stepped aside to let him pass. He didn't want to. He had found his way to the door and seen her and told her, but he didn't want to go in.

"I have to go," he said, then hurried away, stumbling

to reach the castle's ramparts and get up high. He climbed up and up into the blinding sun and found a place to sit where there were no shadows at all.

He must have fallen asleep, for he awoke suddenly with a burning thirst and his heart thumping and pounding as he felt in his pocket for the roll of bills. It was there, but he shook his head — he couldn't expect such luck twice. The streets were busy now. A busload of tourists crowded the pavements, their long fair legs bare in the hot sun. They were buying faked coins and little brass trinkets and bargaining excitedly and holding up their fingers to show how much they would pay. Then they all went over to the parapet and exclaimed at the view and called to each other, jostling and raising their arms and pointing with their large bony hands. He didn't know if they were pointing to the thousands and thousands of roofs of the shantytowns or whether they looked beyond to where the great plain stretched away. That was where he wanted to go — back over those plains. Nobody was going to turn him away and make him bend lower and lower. He started to work his way down through the crowds that were thronging up the hill.

··{ 13 }··

B Y THE TIME he got over to the horse market, his plan was almost clear in his head. He had to walk only a little bit to find the very horse that he wanted. She was a small chestnut mare, with a way of arching her neck and holding her head a little to one side that was pretty. You could not have called her a beautiful horse, not with her sloping shoulders and dirty, winter coat still on her. But she didn't start away from him, and though she was thin, she did not look as though she had been badly treated. He loitered and listened while the seller tried to pass her off as a three-year-old to a man looking for a horse to pull a milk cart.

"She must have been feeding on stones to get her teeth down like that," the man muttered. It was clear that she was no three-year-old. Mehmet pretended to be interested in the big black horse beside her, but he watched carefully as they trotted out the chestnut mare. He wondered why she was for sale, but then reflected that times were so hard that people often had no choice. They sold their children sometimes. He told the man that his father had sent him to buy a big horse to pull in double harness, and the fellow scratched his chin and knocked the price down on the black. Mehmet pretended to have almost decided and gave the black a friendly slap that sent it quivering and shying into the horses beside it.

"Needs a steady hand and a hand that isn't afraid to use the whip," the seller said, for he would dearly have liked to get rid of the black; it was a mean beast and had bitten him the other day. He reduced the price — just for Mehmet, he said. And Mehmet started to feel around in his clothes for the money. It was a trick he had learned from Muhlis.

"And her, what do you want for a little thing like her?" he asked, barely nodding at the little mare.

"You could have her for 200,000 *lira*, though I wouldn't advise it. She won't go in a double harness with a big horse."

"I dunno," said Mehmet, looking stupid.

"It's no good your father coming round tomorrow and saying she don't match," grumbled the man, but Mehmet was counting out the money. He did it very slowly, laying the bills loosely, so that the bundle looked large. Muhlis had always said that people bought more with the eye than the brain. He stopped at 160,000 and then bought her for 175,000, with a blanket and a rope halter thrown in.

When he led her away, he couldn't believe how excited he felt. He was almost afraid to scramble on her back. He'd bought her to harness to the cart. He guessed that she was about the same size as Yıldız. She walked patiently and sometimes pushed her face into his shoulder, and he wondered if he shouldn't try to ride her, just a short way. She was so awkward at first, with her stride short and her shoulders so sloping, that he nearly fell off a couple of times. Then they seemed to get used to each other; she trotted, and then unexpectedly, on the flat ground near the garages and repair shops, she put her head down and started to gallop. With that rope bridle there was no way of stopping her now. The men and boys working on the cars shouted at them and stepped aside, and Mehmet remembered the flat meadows down by the river near his village. That was where the young men galloped their horses. He'd seen them racing there between the two willows. She might not win, but at least she could race. If he got there soon, he could plant one crop of vegetables, and he could lime the fruit trees so that there would be apples and pears in the autumn, though it might be too late for the cherries. It would be enough — nothing special, but enough. With care, the money he had in his pocket should stretch to buy the beginning of a small flock of goats, or perhaps a cow who would calve in the winter. Perhaps he could hire himself out in the summer. People did. They didn't make a fortune, but they didn't starve either. It wasn't like in the town, where you had to pay even for the salad you put in your bread. The little mare had slowed, and though her thick coat was flecked with sweat, she was not whistling or wheezing. He'd get her coat clipped before the hot summer. He'd look after her really well; he wouldn't just wait like his father had done — waiting and hoping and never doing anything until it was too late.

There was a patch of bright green grass sprouting unexpectedly near a cracked water pipe. He slid down from the mare's back and let her graze. There must, after all, have been some reason why their land had dried up. Hayri had talked about it, saying it had to do with cutting down the trees, but Mehmet's father had mocked him. Mehmet had joined in — everybody had joined in; what nonsense, they had said. Trees after all, took water out of the ground, so if you got rid of most of the trees there should be more water left. But perhaps this was another one of those things that they thought they all knew but knew wrong. Maybe you never got to know the answer to some questions, but at least you could ask and listen. He looked up at the sky and thought it had never been so blue.

He tethered the mare out where they had tethered Yıldız, and then in the early evening he went quietly along the paths to Muhlis's house. The cart was still outside, but the harness had gone. Someone had swept the stamped earth in front of the door, he was sure of it. He felt very, very strange. It was as though Muhlis might come ambling out in his odd clothes that were always too small. He pushed the door aside and stopped — there was another family inside; a couple of grown-ups and several children. He recognized them vaguely but didn't know their name.

"Your uncle said that we could, since he's looking after the house," said the woman quickly, defensively. He nodded and backed out again.

"And the harness?"

"He took it with him," she said, eager to have something right to say.

"That's right, I saw him — really I did, really." Mehmet recognized the boy as one of the little ones who had come on the picnic.

"Come and show me, then." He held out his hand, and the little boy ran to him proudly and called to his friends that there was going to be trouble. Freckles came up with his brother and then a group of girls and women with their sewing still in their hands. The children sparred and punched the air and hoped that Mehmet would land a good one. Nobody would have minded seeing Uncle Yusuf and Aunt Fatma made to look foolish, so long as it was not one of their own family that did it.

Aunt Fatma and one or two friends were drinking a late tea in the red room. She came to the door and said, "Why Mehmet, what a surprise! Has your mother sent you?" And she brushed the crumbs from her lips and looked past him to the crowd at the gate. She called at once for Yusuf to come quickly and tried to shut the door, but Mehmet stepped in and was looking into the red room, where the ladies had taken an extra slice of pie while their hostess was gone. He looked into the bedrooms and the kitchen, but no, it wasn't there. His uncle, who was in the middle of his prayers in the sitting room, leaped to his feet and called for the police and other decent citizens to stop this daylight robbery. Mehmet knew he had to find it quickly, for only the crowd beyond the gate kept him safe from his uncle, and they would stay only if he won a swift victory. They would not risk more than a quick laugh, for his benefit. Then he saw it, out in the garden. He and Yusuf got to it at the same time, but Yusuf, in baggy, striped pajamas, seemed conscious that this dispute did him no good. He relaxed his grip, and Mehmet gathered up the long reins, then coiled them, hung the harness over his shoulder, and walked off without having said a single word.

The crowd, with a sense of having seen a sort of justice done, melted away into doorways and down narrow paths, and Mehmet went on alone to the plain. He brought the little mare back to Muhlis's house and there he harnessed her to the cart. He flicked the reins, and the cart's wheels turned so that the faces of the children spun together and the wheels made a faint track back across the dusty earth.

Glossary

abla	elder sister
amca	uncle from father's side of family
ayran	drink made of yogurt and water
bayram	festival or holiday
Bey	Mr.; term of respect added after man's first name
Çinar Sokak	Plane Tree Street
dayı	uncle from mother's side of family
deli	crazy
dolmuş	minibus that takes in many customers and follows a fixed route
gofret	dry, sweet wafer biscuit
gözleme	thin, unleavened bread, like a pancake
Hanım	Mrs.; term of respect added after woman's first name
kahve	café or tea-house; a meeting place for men
Kangal	a breed of shepherd dog used for herding and protecting flocks of sheep and goats
köfte	meatballs
Mevlut	prayers conducted in memory of the dead
şalvar	wide trousers worn by men and women
Şentepe	Happy Hill
simit	hand-size ring of bread, coated with sesame seeds

süzme	strained to remove excess water
teyze	aunt
tornet	wooden pushcart with small iron wheels used for carrying loads
Yenimahalle	place name meaning new neighborhood
yıldız	star
Yokuş Yolu	Steep Way
yorgan	quilt of cotton or wool that has a sheet stitched to the underside

Note regarding spelling and pronunciation of Turkish words:

Ç, ç is pronounced "ch," as in *ch*air
C, c is pronounced "j," as in *J*ohn
Ş, ş is pronounced "sh," as in *sh*oe

In Turkish, the *i* and the *ı* are separate letters:
İ, i is pronounced "i," as in t*i*n
I, ı is pronounced "uh," as in the last syllable of construct*i*on